Written in 1988, *House of America*  has won numerous awards both n. as a play and feature film (1996 *Flowers of the Dead Red Sea* (1991) *Last From The Gantry* (1993) *Song From A Forgotten City* (1995) *Gas Station Angel* (1998) and *Stone City Blue* (2004). Translated into over ten languages the plays have toured widely in the UK, Europe, Australia and South America, at venues including The Royal Court, Donmar Warehouse and Tramway Glasgow. Ed is founder member and creative director of TV production company Fiction Factory and is currently working on *HINTERLAND/ Y GWYLL*, a detective series produced in English and Welsh for S4C, BBC and distributed internationally by All3Media. Over the last ten years, Ed has written, directed or produced more than one hundred and twenty hours of drama across most genres, attracting more than seventy nominations and awards from BAFTA Wales to the Prix Europa and distributed to over eighty countries. His credits include *Satellite City, Silent Village, China, Mind To Kill, Caerdydd, Pen Talar, Y Pris, Cwmgiedd/Columbia* and *Gwaith/Cartref*. He lives in Cardiff.

HOUSE OF AMERICA

Ed Thomas

PARTHIAN

Parthian
The Old Surgery
Napier Street
Cardigan
SA43 1ED
www.parthianbooks.com

This edition published in 2013
© Ed Thomas
All Rights Reserved

ISBN 978-1-906998-54-7

The publisher acknowledges the financial support of the Welsh Books Council.

Cover design by www.theundercard.co.uk
Typeset by Claire Houguez

Printed and bound by lightningsource.com

British Library Cataloguing in Publication Data

A cataloguing record for this book is available from the British Library.

This book is sold subject to the condition that it shall not by way of trade or otherwise be circulated without the publisher's prior consent in any form of binding or cover other than that in which it is published.

CONTENTS

Foreword by David Adams	vii
House of America	1
Pictures	107
Cast Members' Reflections:	
Sharon Morgan	125
Russel Gomer	129
Richard Lynch	131

FOREWORD

DAVID ADAMS TAKES A PERSONAL TRIP BACK TO THE PREMIERE OF THE PLAY

In thirty-odd years of going to theatre in Wales, there is still one event which is seared into my memory. The premiere of *House of America* in May 1988 had an immediate effect on me like no other play I can think of.

That first production, by brand-new company Y Cwmni at St Stephens Theatre Space in Cardiff's Butetown, grabbed me by the throat, shook me, swept me along a rollercoaster ride and had that urgency that, for a theatre critic, is heaven-sent. I came out of Moving Being's converted church not only exhilarated but bursting to tell anyone who'd listen about this amazing experience. Writing my review for *The Guardian* on the train home was more of an exercise in containing my excitement and involvement within the specified word limits than searching for something to say.

And while that original production, directed by Ed Thomas and with Russ Gomer, Tim Lyn, Richard Lynch, Sharon Morgan, Catherine Tregenna and Wyndham Price, relied on its outstanding performances, I did indeed spend much of my professional life talking about this remarkable play, even as a written text. In fact I was positively evangelical about it.

Any theatre commentator working in Wales at the time would use *House of America* as a point of reference and I certainly depended on it in my mission to celebrate wherever I could the new radical performance work coming out of Wales – work over the next decade or so like that from Brith Gof, Volcano Theatre and Earthfall, from performers like Eddie Ladd, Marc Rees and Sioned Huws, from playwrights like Ian Rowlands, Greg Cullen and Dic Edwards – and the incredible output of Ed Thomas.

I tried to watch all subsequent productions of *House of America*. I caught it in community venues during its tour a few months after the St Stephens opening, I saw it in Chapter at the end of the year. When it went to London I persuaded *Time Out* magazine to print a feature from me on the company and the playwright; *Time Out* was to honour it with the *Time Out*/01 for London new play award. I caught Jamie Garven's radical redirection in 1992 (where Lisa Palfrey took over as Gwenny and made the role her own, reprising it, albeit less effectively, in the later film). I was intrigued by the 1996 movie version, which importantly re-orientated the play's direction, and I enjoyed with some reservations the subsequent new stage version from Ed that had more than a nod to the film script

Ten years after its premiere it still loomed large for me. I had, I guess, become an Ed Thomas groupie.

When I organised a small (but ground-breaking) Welsh arts festival in Zagreb in 1999, I insisted we took not only *House of America* but Ed Thomas. Ed and I appeared on Croatian breakfast-time tv and did a chaotic Q&A in front of an audience that included the national culture minister (whose only question at the end was "What is this 'sheep-shagging' you referred to, Mr Thomas?"). The play text, in Croatian, was printed along with an extensive article on theatre in Wales in the leading arts magazine *Kazaliste* in 2000.

The key set-text in a course I ran at Warwick University in the mid-2000s on Theatre and National Identity was *House of America*, where the third-year students simply couldn't understand why they had neither read it nor seen this impressive piece of theatre before.

A couple of years later, in the autumn of 2006, when I curated a season of Welsh theatre for Michael Kelligan's On the Edge season at Chapter, I invited over a Macedonian director, Dean Damjonovski, to interpret *House of America* from a different perspective (some British theatre was seen as very radical in central Europe, where the less naturalistic work around the Royal Court was all the rage).

So, yes, it had an impact on me and I made sure that I passed on that wherever I could.

I would, of course, never suggest I was the only one to see the qualities of *House of America* and the promise of its author: it was taken up by the Royal Court in London, where it received the 1989 *Time Out* award for best new play, for example. Ed Thomas's name started being mentioned along with other new playwrights like David Greig and Martin Crimp. The Royal Court went on to commission and co-produce Ed's *Song from a Forgotten City* in 1995 and *Gas Station Angel* in 1998 (the last Welsh play to be commissioned by the Court).

Today *House of America* has, surely, become an English-language Welsh-theatre classic. No, there isn't much of a choice: but it ranks up there along with *Taffy*, *Under Milk Wood* and *Cardiff East*. It is also one of the few Welsh plays to have been performed internationally, having been seen in Australia, Belgium, Canada, Croatia, Germany, Romania, Spain, Ukraine and elsewhere.

There are several reasons why *House of America* became so important to Welsh theatre. It is, for a start, a thoughtful, well-written play by a writer who was also an actor: it has good dialogue that goes from farce to tragedy and has some cracking roles. It is unlike any play that had gone before, the only comparison being Glyn Thomas's *The Keep*, which also dealt with a family imprisoned in their house.

But, crucially, Ed Thomas in his first play reinvented state-of-the-nation drama.

Plays that set themselves the task of negotiating ideas of national identity had been with us since Wales had an independent theatrical practice, from the early days of J O Francis's 1913 *Change* and Caradoc Evans's *Taffy* in 1923.

Not all plays written in Wales are about being Welsh – but it's surprising how many are. Welshness is for many the most important defining characteristic of identity and lies at the heart of a lot of drama here. I think Ed Thomas's success seemed to signal a coming-out of Welsh state-of-the-nation playwrights: eloquent, angry, frustrated writers like Ian Rowlands and, to a lesser extent, Patrick Jones poetically vented their spleen on stage, and new writers like Gary Owen and Aled Jones Williams in their different ways entered the debate, while established writers like Frank Vickery and Meic Povey found themselves being reinterpreted; in the medium of Welsh, Gareth Miles's hard-edged political plays seemed even more relevant.

In the decade after *House of America*, Ed Thomas's work continued to explore the 'New Wales': *Flowers of the Dead Red Sea, Adar Heb Adenydd/ The Myth of Michael Roderick, East from the Gantry, Hiraeth/ Strangers in Conversation, Envy, Song for a Forgotten City*, which won the 1995 Barclays New Stages Award. The last of this impressive output was *Gas Station Angel*, which in June 1998 opened, like *Song for a Forgotten City*, at the Royal Court in London.

Thereafter Ed Thomas collaborated with Mike Pearson of the by then defunct Brith Gof in *Rain Dogs* (2002) and wrote

Stone City Blue (2004) for Clwyd Theatr Cymru, neither of which could be seen as part of that 'New Wales' agenda. By the time we get to *Stone City Blue*, Ed Thomas's last produced play, the search for Welsh cultural identity looked to have been redundant, abandoned, exhausted.

House of America, meanwhile, was translated into at least half-a-dozen languages. Y Cwmni transmogrified into Fiction Factory, which restaged the play and toured it nationally and to Australia in 1997-1998.

For anyone in Wales, and to an extent in regions seeking self-determination, from Quebec to Catalonia, the politics of the play was self-evident. It is the American Dream as imagined by a dysfunctional Welsh trio of siblings with underneath a nightmare about self-deception, secrets and lies, lack of confidence, and the question of family and nationhood that was one complex metaphor for a country that had recently voted against independence from England and had to reinvent itself. Anyone who had read Gwyn Alf Williams's brilliant *When Was Wales?* would have understood immediately what this fiery, fervent young man was writing about: published in 1985, Professor Williams's book was a radical questioning of Welsh identity through history, a story of rupture and reinvention.

For others, however, especially those who preferred theatre not have an agenda, it was something else – a Sam Shepard style domestic drama, perhaps, or word-heavy lyrical rant, not unlike that other Thomas, Dylan, according to some London critics. There were those who picked up on the intellectually-fashionable postmodernist themes of memory and identity and the slipperiness of meaning.

For others it was a Greek tragedy transposed to a disintegrating, despairing, disordered dystopia, its story of incest and fratricide driving a claustrophobic narrative of communal self-immolation.

For those more used to mythic, violent, angst-ridden tragedy, its political and its domestic setting were transparent smokescreens for an epic confrontation with fate and mankind's inner nature. The critical comment from Dean Damjonovski in 2006, when he directed it for the State of the Nation season at Chapter Arts Centre, goes some way to explaining the play's popularity in Eastern Europe: 'Edward Thomas overcomes the socio-cultural context and reaches all the way to the mythological-ritual nature of the Human,' wrote the Macedonian director. 'Metaphorically speaking it reaches to the roots of Evil.' That's a very European interpretation and is evidenced in their productions of tragedies from Shakespeare to Sara Kane.

So here we are again, a quarter of a century after it first appeared, and I am revisiting that night down in Cardiff Bay, trying to recreate the impact this small-scale theatre event had in 1988 – without the foreknowledge of Ed Thomas's subsequent playwriting career or the development of Welsh theatre.

There are many who would say that that production of *House of America* in St Stephen's Theatre Space changed the face of Welsh theatre. For we historians of Welsh theatre that may be in a way true and those involved in Welsh theatre, whether practitioners, audiences or critics, quite possibly were to judge other work against the achievements of *House of America*. But there were no copycat plays: Ed Thomas is quite unique.

What it did do was give a relatively fledgling art form, English-language Welsh theatre, a profile. Here at last was a work which made audiences and critics sit up and take notice.

The play and its author seemed to come, as it were, out of the blue.

I had been reviewing theatre in Wales since 1979: the year of the Referendum that saw a nation vote against having its own government and of the advent of Thatcherism with a massive swing against Labour in Wales, two traumas that also served as stimuli for much that followed in the arts. The miners' fights and the running-down of the steel industry in the 1980s helped define the era.

At first there was little discernable reaction and the innovations in Welsh theatre were not in playwriting. The radical Danish-based 'third theatre' collective, Odin Teatret, toured the country in 1980 and a year later as a consequence the legendary Brith Gof was formed by members of Cardiff Laboratory Theatre. Moving Being had moved from London to Cardiff, initially to Chapter Arts Centre before moving to St Stephens, and in 1981 produced *Y Mabinogi* in the grounds of Cardiff Castle. Volcano Theatre, probably the company that made the most impact outside Wales, introduced us in 1983 to their idiosyncratic style of physical theatre that was premised on an academic socialism that felt at home in a traditionally left-wing Wales. The Magdalena Project, to become the most international of Welsh theatre companies, was launched in 1986.

But there were some important moves in more traditional drama, crucially the formation in 1981 of *Made in Wales*, dedicated to new plays. Writers like Alan Osborne, Laurence Allan, Dic Edwards, Tim Rhys and Ian Rowlands were taken under its wing – as, for his first performed plays, was Ed Thomas. *When the River Runs Dry*, a forty-minute piece written while Ed was still living in London, was produced in 1986 at the Write On! Festival, where it was changed radically between its two performances at the insistence of the playwright: I can't remember which I saw, but it made an impression, though as far as I know it was never performed again. *The Last Order in the Hope* followed for *Made in Wales* but was never properly finished.

I guess Ed must also have already been working on *The Myth of Michael Roderick*, which didn't actually get a staging until 1990, because a Welsh-language version of it, titled *Adar*

Heb Adenydd, which translates as *Birds Without Wings*, was produced by *Made in Wales* shortly after *House of America*; it was his only play in his native Welsh and deals in surrealistic style with those themes that were to permeate his work – the need for new myths and new heroes.

Made in Wales declined to commission Ed Thomas further; it could have been they that gave us *House of America*, but it wasn't and instead a group of Welsh-speaking actors formed Y Cwmni.

So Ed Thomas and *House of America* burst upon us when theatre in Wales was at the time feeling more exciting than ever before. Indeed it was as part of Watch This Space!, a radical writing season produced by Geoff Moore of Moving Being at St Stephens, that the newly-formed Y Cwmni staged *House of America*. (Eddie Ladd, then performing under her own name of Gwyneth Owen, was a startling Juliet in Geoff Moore's own *Romeo and Juliet* in the St Stephens 1986 Shakespeare Season.) The production a few months later toured Welsh community venues and ended up at Chapter Arts Centre - and then went to London, which until a year or so before had been Ed's home.

House of America had probably been written for a while – it reflected to an extent the writer's obsessions while in voluntary exile in London and is to an extent, too, a play written at a distance from its subject – which is perhaps why Ed never liked it as much as his subsequent plays. It is also written in 'heightened realism' – the first and last.

But for those of us in the audience at St Stephens (and I can even remember exactly where I sat, even, and that I was in an audience of single figures) it was a real shock to the system, even if you'd caught the Write On! pieces.

Here Ed Thomas articulated what was perhaps there already in Wales, not only an awareness that industrial heritage was being destroyed and massive unemployment and misery created as a result, but a feeling of insecurity, an identity crisis, a need for reinvention. For example, *House of America* was not the first Welsh play to deal with issues like entrapment: *The Keep* was a notable precursor, with its family trapped a metaphor for a nation appropriated and confined by its oppressive neighbour. Perhaps that desire but inability to escape was part of the Welsh psyche, and it was present in much subsequent theatre, particularly in Gary Owen's *Crazy Gary's Mobile Disco* some dozen years later.

And Ed Thomas's plays are not simply about 'cultural identity': they are about family, the author, memory, myth, madness, nation, language and many other elements that make the idea of 'identity' very complex.

But it was initially the exciting theatricality of the production that made the audience reel. Nothing this arresting, this eloquent, this electric had ever been seen on the Welsh stage – it was comparable, I suppose, to *Look Back in Anger*'s premier on the London stage in 1956, at the Royal Court, of course, which was to stage *House of America* in 1989. What made the play endure was that underlying the theatricality was a passion, an intelligence, an anger – and, crucially, perhaps a despair that only dissipated when that 1979 Referendum vote was reversed in 1997 and the hated Tories sent packing.

Ironically it was then, in 1997, less than a decade after the explosion rocked Welsh theatre, that not only Ed Thomas's creative run of plays dried up but Welsh theatre itself was in the doldrums – and I don't think it ever really recovered.

Today Ed Thomas concentrates on the impressively large TV output of Fiction Factory – *Hinterland/ Y Gwyll*, based in Aberystwyth, is being produced for BBC and S4C in English and Welsh, a major breakthrough. *House of America* is still produced, but mainly by students, although a Welsh-language version (translation by that first Mam, Sharon Morgan) was produced by Theatr Genedlaethol Cymru in 2010.

Ed Thomas has lost none of his creativity or his politics but has written nothing for the stage since *Stone City Blue*, though he still would not like to feel he has given up theatre work. He has been commissioned by the National Theatre of Wales to adapt Brecht's *Mother Courage* and then, who knows, may surprise us all again. His imagination, his idealism, his distinct voice is as desperately needed as much as it was a quarter of a century ago, in 1988, when we staggered into the Butetown early summer night knowing we had just witnessed something utterly remarkable and unforgettable.

David Adams
2013

HOUSE OF AMERICA

House of America was first performed in May, 1988, at St Stephen's Theatre, Cardiff, as part of their radical writing season, with the following cast:

Mam	Sharon Morgan
Gwenny	Catherine Tregenna
Boyo	Tim Lyn
Sid	Russel Gomer
Labourer	Wyndham Price

Music by	Wyndham Price
Set and Lighting by	Ian Hill
Directed by	Edward Thomas

The revised version toured South Wales, London and the Edinburgh Festival in 1989, with Richard Lynch playing the role of Boyo.

ACT ONE

(*Velvet Underground's 'Here She Comes' plays as* GWENNY, SID *and* BOYO *play boisterously. Music fades.* MOTHER *enters.*)

MOTHER: Thing is with a story is that you've got to be sure of the facts, or people will only get the wrong end of the stick, and you end up upsetting people without meaning to. I didn't mean any harm you say, but it's too late, the damage is done. Then with some stories there's so much going on you don't know where to start, like if I tell you what happened the night Clem, my husband, left me. He went to America, that's the simple way of saying it, but there's more to it than that. Clem's a lorry driver you see, well I don't know if he is now, haven't seen him in years, or heard from him. I remember him telling me one day the steering on the lorry went on the way to north Wales. 'It's all the bends you see,' he said. 'Bend after bend, what I want is a straight road, America's got straight roads see, you get on and you never have to get off.' It was the steering in his head that was gone, not the lorry. He said, 'I want a new life in a house by the sea in California.' I said 'You don't have to go to California to find a house by the sea, there's places here, in Wales.' And he said, 'Yeah, I know, but there's no room to park the lorry.' Funny the things you remember on the day your husband leaves you. It had been one of those days, I'd been using the washing machine, but we had this cat see, called Brando, that was Clem's idea, Clem thought the world of Marlon Brando, but what I thought was funny was Marlon Brando had never heard of Clem. Anyway, when my back was turned, the cat decided to have a nap in the washing machine, and I didn't know it was in there, so I shut the door and started the machine, you can guess what happened, the cat couldn't swim. All of a sudden Clem came in, he loved the cat so I didn't know what to tell him, and I was just about to say something when he said 'I'm off', or something like that, and I said 'What do you mean off?' 'I'm going to America' he said 'tonight.' And I said 'Oh.' He was looking at me dumb, and said, 'Well? What have you got to say?' 'Brando's dead,' I said, 'I've just washed him to death. He got into the washing machine when I wasn't looking, it was an accident.' 'You did it on purpose,' he said. 'I'm definitely going.' 'I put him over there in the Tesco bag,' I said. 'He's still wet.' Clem just looked at me and turned to go, and I said 'What about the kids?' 'Keep them away from the washing machine.' And he shut the door behind him. I haven't seen him since. So it was just me and the kids left, I told them where he'd gone and left it at that. Then I buried the cat down the bottom of the garden with a lollipop stick as a cross, buried him next to budgie Billy. You have to make do, see.

(*Loud crashing, blasting noise. Stops.*)

They're starting an open cast mine, it's enough to frighten any bugger.

(*Music of Dionne Warwick singing 'Do you know the way to San Jose' as* MOTHER *exits.* BOYO *and* GWENNY *race in and build a house of cards.*)

GWENNY: You ever heard of someone called Joyce Johnson, Boyo?

BOYO: No , should I?

GWENNY: Not really, no.

BOYO: What she about then?

GWENNY: No, I was just wondering.

BOYO: How's the cards coming on?

GWENNY: Not good, there's too much of a draught, see, look they're shaking.

BOYO: I know, the house is facing north, bound to get a draught.

GWENNY: That's got nothing to do with it, all I know is that now and then the draught blows, and rocks all the cards at the bottom of the pack, here, look, so they're all shakey, so the next card you put on is bound to bring the lot down, so you can't build on it, watch now.

(GWENNY *carefully puts a card on. It wobbles a bit and they fall down.* BOYO *laughs.*)

GWENNY: See what I mean.

BOYO: It's not the wind mun, it's the table, it's wonky.

GWENNY: I'm telling you it's a draught, I can feel it.

(BOYO *watches as she starts again.*)

GWENNY: It's not going to beat me though.

(BOYO *walks around half-heartedly looking for a draught. He picks up a book.*)

BOYO: This your book?

GWENNY: Yeah, well no…

BOYO: Uh?

GWENNY: It's Sid's, but he lent it to me.

BOYO: Jesus, he hasn't read a book in years, has he?

GWENNY: Don't know, but he likes that one.

BOYO: What's this bloke called… Jack…

GWENNY: Kerouac.

BOYO: Never heard of him.

GWENNY: He's from America.

BOYO: '…The Beat Generation's classic novel of sex, jazz and freedom.' Sounds alright to me, I knew Sid liked two of them, one he doesn't get very often and another one he thinks he's got, but I didn't know he liked jazz.

GWENNY: He does, and I do, but he hasn't got the money to buy the records.

BOYO: News to me.

GWENNY: He went to Brecon Jazz Festival last year remember?

BOYO: Oh yeah, but I thought he went because of the booze, and a lift on a motorbike.

GWENNY: No, he likes music too. Charlie Parker he likes. You can borrow the book after me Boyo.

BOYO: Yeah, I'll have to. (*Throws down the book.*)

GWENNY: He'll be back before long now… hope he gets those jobs for you.

BOYO: What jobs?

GWENNY: The ones on the new open cast. They want labourers, local labourers, Sid's gone to see some Irish bloke about it.

BOYO: Jesus, why didn't he tell me then?

GWENNY: I thought he did.

BOYO: Been telling you all his secrets has he?

(GWENNY *looks away.*)

GWENNY: He told me he thought he was getting old before his time.

BOYO: That's my fault that is, I told him his hair was falling out and his teeth needed filling.

(*The card house collapses again.*)

Oh. Christ, look its happened again.

(BOYO *laughs.*)

GWENNY: That's it. I've had enough.

BOYO: Hey, I don't want any jibs.

GWENNY: I'm not jibbing.

(GWENNY *takes a chair and stands on it looking out the window.* BOYO *takes over with the cards.*)

GWENNY: What would happen if all the planets round the sun slow down then, Boyo?

BOYO: Hey, mun, what sort of question is that?

GWENNY: Heard it on the radio I did, the earth is travelling at eighteen miles a second round the sun.

BOYO: How many potatoes were made into chips last year – keeps you awake at nights doesn't it?

GWENNY: But, if all the planets… like Earth right, decide to slow down, well, we'd just fall into the sun and burn.

BOYO: I'd better keep my fingers crossed then or pray to Jesus or something.

MOTHER: Jesus is a busy man.

BOYO: Uh?

(MOTHER *appears at the back of the stage.*)

MOTHER: I said Jesus is a busy man, you can't always get through to him when you call, but he knows me. I say 'Jesus, it's Mrs. Lewis from Wales', and if I'm lucky, on a good night he'll answer. Was it you who wanted him Boyo?

BOYO: No, me and Gwenny was just talking.

MOTHER: Like I got through to him the other night, asking forgiveness, but I wasn't at my best, but you know what he said, he said there was so much going on down there it's hard to keep track, and if it carried on like this he'd have to go and put his head in the sand, Jesus himself.

BOYO: Well, if he feels like that what have we got to worry about, innit, uh, Gwen?

GWENNY: Oh, yeah… yeah…

MOTHER: I mean with all those things on his mind he could hit the bottle, and we can't have him drunk in charge of the world, can we?

BOYO: What you want him to forgive you for then?

MOTHER: That's between him, me, and the deep blue sea. Doing tricks, Boyo?

(*She knocks the cards over.*)

BOYO: Oi, mun, what you want to do that for? I was getting somewhere then.

MOTHER: I want to talk.

GWENNY: What about?

MOTHER: My room's been painted blue.

BOYO: So?

MOTHER: It's the wrong colour.

GWENNY: It's been blue for as long as I can remember, Mam.

MOTHER: Nobody painted it behind my back then?

BOYO: No, what do you think?

MOTHER: Don't make fun. I wouldn't have asked if I didn't think it.

GWENNY: You probably painted it yourself, Mam.

MOTHER: It's the wrong colour I say. Red's my colour. If it had been painted red nobody'd see the dirt. It's the open cast, it's the worst that could have happened here. If anybody goes to the shop buy some red paint for my room, got to be red. Damn open cast.

(BOYO *and* GWENNY *exchange glances.*)

BOYO: It's here now, so that's that.

GWENNY: And the boys need jobs.

MOTHER: Wet behind the ears, the two of you.

BOYO: Hey listen, I'm not going to argue. Oh, the bastard thing's fallen again.

GWENNY: I don't know what you're bothering for tonight Boyo, you'll never do it.

MOTHER: It'll change everything.

(*Fade in Sam and Dave's 'Soul Man' as* SID *enters exuberantly.*)

MOTHER: Turn the music down, I'm trying to talk.

(*No response. Eventually she goes to the record player herself and turns the music off.*)

SID: Hey mun, I was getting into that.

MOTHER: How old are you?

SID: What sort of question is that, Mother?

MOTHER: You're nearly thirty, and I'm trying to talk.

SID: Hey come on, not now, not now, I've got news.

MOTHER: What news?

SID: News... News... News.

GWENNY: What Sid, what?

SID: Boyo, me and you are going to Hirwaun in that

three-legged car of yours to sign up for jobs as labourers, and the money, brother, is sweet.

BOYO: Hey, Sid that's great.

GWENNY: Great.

BOYO: What time have we got to be there?

SID: First thing in the morning.

GWENNY: What time's that?

SID: I don't know, nine o'clock I suppose.

BOYO: I'll have to put the alarm on.

SID: Five years' work, then they fill the hole in, plant some grass and trees and you can't tell anybody's been there, and then fly across the sea.

GWENNY: We can go to America on that.

SID: Too right we can, c'mon, who fancies a pint, celebrate it? Gwenny, you coming?

BOYO: We'll have a job each now.

MOTHER: Women were his weakness. He didn't smoke, didn't drink much and he couldn't help the way he looked. Everybody thought he was handsome, didn't have much of a temper, just had a soft spot for women, that was his trouble.

SID: What she talking about now, for Christ's sake?

MOTHER: Your father, who do you think I'm talking about?

BOYO: What's he got to do with anything now?

SID: C'mon, let's go, she's only having a rant.

MOTHER: Looked like a film star he did, like Errol Flynn. I was lucky, I've told Mr. Snow all about him.

GWENNY: Mr Snow?

SID: Who's he?

MOTHER: Haven't I told you about Mr Snow?

BOYO: No, you…

MOTHER: She was a floozy… your father ran away with a floozy. I was too busy looking after you three, he always said I had no time for him, and then the floozy got her hands on him behind my back. He was a dreamer and he fell for the glitter.

GWENNY: It's all right, Mam.

MOTHER: No, it's not all right, the open cast will dig up everything in sight, and I'll be lost. Let sleeping dogs lie, it's been a long time, history is history.

BOYO: What you trying to say, Mam?

MOTHER: But I've already told you haven't I? He's in America, you know he's in America, don't you?

GWENNY: Yes.

BOYO: Where else is he then, Mam?

MOTHER: Nowhere… that's where he went to, left us in the lurch, wasn't my fault, could have happened to anyone, but mind you this is where he belongs… but he couldn't see, this was his home but he didn't know, and he'll come back here one day.

GWENNY: You think so?

MOTHER: Definite, he won't be in America forever, liked John Wayne too much he did, so he went to the Wild West with his floozy.

SID: Frontier man the old man see, Boyo, took his whore and his woman, headed West and built a ranch for himself.

(SID *laughs*.)

BOYO: Shut up mun, Sid, don't wind her up.

MOTHER: She had relations out there…you talking behind my back?

SID: No, no, just saying to Boyo, that's right I said.

GWENNY: C'mon, Mam, come and have a lie down, you'll feel better then.

MOTHER; You're not going to work on the open cast, are you?

SID: Yeah…interview's tomorrow.

MOTHER: You can't, hear me, you can't, it'll be the end of us.

SID: It's a job. A job is a job.

MOTHER: Listen to you, still boys.

SID: Hey, I'm pushing thirty.

BOYO: He's only pulling your leg, Mam, all the jobs have gone. Here, let Gwenny take you for a lie down.

MOTHER: I don't trust you boys, you're not listening to me.

GWENNY: C'mon, Mam.

(GWENNY *leads* MOTHER *away*.)

MOTHER: I'm warning you.

(MOTHER *and* GWENNY *exit*.)

SID: She's getting worse.

BOYO: It's just her nerves, that's all.

SID: The men in white coats will be knocking on the door and taking her away if she's not careful.

BOYO: She's not that bad yet, we'll have to keep an eye on her.

SID: What she bring the old man up for now?

BOYO: I don't know.

SID: Maybe she's heard from him.

BOYO: How?

SID: I don't know, written her a letter or something.

BOYO: Why should he bother now when we haven't heard a peep from him since he went?

SID: You never know.

BOYO: I haven't seen any letters.

SID: Hey, he might be writing to ask us to go out there on a visit.

BOYO: Bollocks to him, I wouldn't go.

SID: You're off your head, big country, mun, get a job

there and settle down.

BOYO: We don't even know where he lives, mun.

SID: Fuck, a trip to America, be all right I reckon.

BOYO: Might be for you, but I don't see it that way.

SID: Don't be so miserable, mun, it's only an idea.

BOYO: Where's he been for the last ten years, that's what I want to know. If he thought anything of us he'd have written earlier, as it stands now he can drop dead. I don't ever want to see the bastard, fuck him and fuck America.

SID: Don't get so heavy, mun, things change, got to change with the times, Boyo, got to give him a chance, he's our old man, mun.

BOYO: What chance did he give us, Sid, uh?

SID: That was a long time ago, we've all grown up now, and he probably had his reasons.

(*Lights fade on* BOYO *and* SID. *Lights up on* MOTHER *and* GWENNY *on another part of the stage.*)

MOTHER: Do you know who you are?

GWENNY: Yes, Mam, Gwenny.

MOTHER: Do you know who I am?

GWENNY: You're my mother.

MOTHER: And what's a mother, Gwenny?

GWENNY: You are.

MOTHER: Are you sure? Have I done a good job, have I

brought you up all right?

GWENNY: Yes, course you have.

MOTHER: Things aren't right, is it me?

GWENNY: No mam.

MOTHER: Do you know what home is?

GWENNY: Yes.

MOTHER: What is it?

GWENNY: It's where we live, Mam, all of us.

MOTHER: Where is it?

GWENNY: Here, where do you think it is?

MOTHER: I've done my best, you know I've done my best, don't you? Everything I did was to help you three.

GWENNY: Mam, I…

MOTHER: No more, leave me alone now, I'm all right.

GWENNY: Mam… I can…

MOTHER: Leave me alone, I need time to think.

(MOTHER *exits.* GWENNY *rejoins* SID *and* BOYO.)

SID: She all right now?

GWENNY: Her nerves are really bad.

BOYO: Playing tricks with her mind.

SID: Listen to Doctor Quack here.

BOYO: Could happen.

GWENNY: I thought she'd be glad to see you getting some work.

SID: Rambling she is, she'll be all right in a bit. Who's coming down the pub?

BOYO: Bit awkward now, innit? One of us will have to stay and look after her.

GWENNY: Don't look at me, it's always me.

SID: I'm dying of thirst.

BOYO: We can't leave her on her own, mun.

GWENNY: He's right Sid, we'll all have to stay.

SID: That's typical, that's fucking typical.

BOYO: She can't help being ill, mun.

SID: Putting it on she is, I'm telling you, any excuse to keep us in the house. We're not youngsters for Christ sake.

GWENNY: We can't leave her whether she's joking or not.

SID: She always comes up with something to put the mockers on things, a Spaniard in the works.

BOYO: Don't be a bastard, Sid, will you?

SID: Celebration this is supposed to be, when was the last time you heard of jobs coming up?

BOYO: That's not the point, is it?

SID: I'm just saying aren't I?

GWENNY: C'mon, there's no point arguing about it, why don't we go down the off-licence and get some cans instead, then we'll have a little party, and we can look after her.

SID: Give that woman an O' level. Gwenny, I love you. Put some pennies on the table.

(BOYO *laughs.*)

BOYO: You're a bastard, aren't you?

SID: C'mon, Boyo, put your cash on the table.

GWENNY: Who's going down then?

SID: I'll go, and someone else to give me a hand.

GWENNY: I'll go, I wouldn't mind a walk.

BOYO: Hey, buy some Jaffa Cakes too. I wouldn't mind some Jaffa Cakes.

SID: See what we can do, brother.

(SID *and* GWENNY *exit.* BOYO *lights a cigarette and goes to stamd at the window.* MOTHER *appears in the shadows and watches him.*)

MOTHER: See anything special out there, Boyo?

BOYO: Oh, I didn't hear you… yeah… have a look.

MOTHER: What's out there?

BOYO: There's a sheep out there look, limping.

MOTHER: Where?

BOYO: Down there look, by the fence, – it's hopping around.

MOTHER: It's lost, that's what it is.

BOYO: Can't keep up with the flock when you've got three legs, can you? The farmer'll send it to the slaughterhouse, won't he?

MOTHER: Not if it's going to lamb, he'll wait for her to lamb and then get rid of her.

BOYO: Hard life being a sheep, innit? (*Laughs.*)

(*Pause.* MOTHER *studies him.*)

MOTHER: Do you love me, Boyo?

BOYO: Uh?

MOTHER: You heard.

BOYO: What you asking me that for?

MOTHER: I want to know.

BOYO: Yeah…

MOTHER: I want to hear you say it.

BOYO: Oh come on, mun, give me a break.

MOTHER: I want to hear you say it.

BOYO: I love you, all right. You're my mother.

MOTHER: You're not going to forget about me, are you?

BOYO: No, what do you think?

MOTHER: I wouldn't have asked you if I knew.

BOYO: Well you know now, right?

MOTHER: So you're not going to send me away.

BOYO: What do we want to do that for?

MOTHER: Because my mind's not right, my nerves are bad, you know they are, I'm not myself.

BOYO: I know that, but you'll get better, this is your home, mun, this is where you belong.

MOTHER: Would you still love me if you knew I'd done something wrong, something bad?

BOYO: Yeah, course I would.

MOTHER: No matter what it was?

BOYO: I'd know you had your reasons.

MOTHER: Good boy.

BOYO: Why did you ask?

MOTHER: I wanted to be sure.

(*Pause.*)

Listen, you've got to promise me something.

BOYO: What?

MOTHER: You and your brother. I don't want you to work on that open cast.

BOYO: Oh, come on now. It's work, Mam, it won't come that near the house, they're only digging the mountains, they don't want the house as well. Is that what you're afraid of?

MOTHER: This house is all we've got, you just said, I heard you.

BOYO: Coal they want, not houses.

MOTHER: Your history, part of your history is on that mountain.

BOYO: I know.

MOTHER: It's lying there, quiet, not making any noise, they'll start digging, and that will be that – all hell will break loose. Huh, this house is full of lies, but I suppose it's kept us together.

BOYO: What lies?

MOTHER: It's kept us together and that's the main thing, you told me yourself, and now they're going to dig the mountains and the mountains are full of lies and this house will start rocking, and I'm telling you, Boyo, you'll have to be strong, you'll have to remember who you are and where you are, and as long as you've got that you'll be all right but you've got to stick together, you listening?

BOYO: What you telling me for?

MOTHER: Because I've been watching you, Gwenny and Sid. I know they want to go to America after him but there's nothing there, and Gwenny's been writing him letters.

BOYO: How do you know?

MOTHER: I've got eyes, I can see you're on my side, I heard you call your father a bastard, you said it tonight. Do you think I haven't got ears?

BOYO: Yeah, on the side of your head by the looks of it.

MOTHER: (*Grabs him.*) Don't laugh at your mother.

BOYO: I'm not laughing, leave me go.

(MOTHER *leaves him go.*)

BOYO: What's my father got to do with it?

MOTHER: Everything. He's not in America, he's never been to America, all he ever did was dream about America.

BOYO: Everybody knows he went to America.

MOTHER: Lies, all lies. It was the only way to keep us together.

BOYO: Then where the hell is he?

(*Silence.*)

Mam? Answer me?

MOTHER: I was only joking. You'll have to be strong, and you said you'll always love me and I believe you.

BOYO: Where is he, Mam?

(MOTHER *kisses him.*)

MOTHER: Don't tell your brother and sister, not yet, but the time will come, you'll have to be strong.

BOYO: Tell me where he is.

MOTHER: You told me you didn't know who Mr Snow was, well I'll tell you. Some people call him interference, you know? On the telly. But I call him Mr Snow.

(MOTHER *walks off.*)

BOYO: Oh Jesus…

(*Lights change. BOYO, SID and GWENNY are drinking, in a party state. The Doors 'Love Her Madly' plays in the background.*)

BOYO: I'm telling you, Sid, John Cale never played with the Doors, he was with Velvet Underground, ask Gwenny.

GWENNY: Boyo's right, Sid, Velvet Underground.

SID: Oh balls to it anyway, Lou Reed's better than John Cale. *I said, hey babe, take a walk on the wild side.*

GWENNY: I'm dancing on my own, who's going to dance?

BOYO: I can't dance, or I'll hic… fall over.

(*Laughter.*)

BOYO: Hey, the other thing about John Cale was, he's Welsh.

SID: No, he's not, he's American, New York band.

BOYO: I'm telling you he comes from Ponty or somewhere.

SID: Bullshit, Boyo, talking crap.

BOYO: You ask Cat next time you see him.

SID: What does he know?

BOYO: He's fucking tuned the piano for Lindisfarne, that's what he knows, last time they were in the Rank in Town.

SID: Aye, but look what happened to them after that, they haven't had a hit since.

BOYO: Not the point, Sid.

SID: Cat, what he does know, the only deaf piano tuner in the country, and I don't care if Cale came from fucking Ystrad, he's living in New York now, and I bet you that's

==where he'll stay, huh, can you imagine Lou Reed walking 'round Ystrad – all right Lou, how's it going on the wild side – not cool enough for him, no way, probably never even heard of Wales.==

BOYO: He don't know nothing that's why.

GWENNY: C'mon, come and dance.

(BOYO *gets up and falls over. General laughter.*)

BOYO: Jesus, my legs have had it, what's that rocket fuel you bought?

(SID *gets up and struggles to dance with* GWENNY, BOYO *mimes a Gerry Anderson puppet, drawing a very wobbly imaginary gun.*)

BOYO: Butteeeeeeeeeaaaaaawwwww.

SID: Quick, Gwenny, duck, the Mysterons are here.

BOYO: (*Singing*) Captain Scarlet, indestructible.

(SID *wobbly shoots back at* BOYO.)

BOYO: Ahh… he got me… (*falls over*) Oi, Sid… Thunderbird one, wus, in trouble.

SID: What you think then, Lady Penelope?

GWENNY: Drive me to the sun, Parker.

SID: Yes, milady.

(SID *picks* GWENNY *up and runs around the room, the music fades and* MOTHER *is standing in the shadows.*)

GWENNY: Oh look, it's Mam. Put me down, Parker.

SID: Yes, milady.

GWENNY: Feeling better?

SID: We're having a party here, are you staying or going, Mam?

MOTHER: What time is it?

BOYO: Not late, Mam, you better?

SID: She's going to stay and have a drink.

MOTHER: Been playing, you three?

GWENNY: Come and sit down here, look, by me.

MOTHER: I came to see about the fire.

SID: Don't worry about the fire, plenty of fire here, hot.

MOTHER: Can't let it go out, needs wood, we'll have to keep it in. I'll go and get some wood.

BOYO: Not now, Mam, can't go out now, and there's plenty of... hic... wood.

SID: See, the fire's happy.

GWENNY: Come and sit here, Mam.

SID: Yeah, we're celebrating. Job interviews tomorrow, mun, have a drink.

(GWENNY *pours* MOTHER *a drink.*)

MOTHER: Is there a film on or what?

SID: A film?

GWENNY: We've been dancing, but you want to see a film.

BOYO: Yeah, go on, Sid, go and put a film on.

SID: Aye, I'm knackered anyway.

GWENNY: Good job we've got a video.

MOTHER: I didn't know we had one, where did it come from?

BOYO: Ask no questions and I'll tell you no lies.

SID: Same place as the ironing board, the camera, Gwenny's jacket…

GWENNY: We don't need a list, Sid.

SID: That's where they all came from.

GWENNY: What sort of film do you want, Mam?

MOTHER: Have you got any musicals?

BOYO: No, Mam, no musicals.

SID: It's all right, problem solved… found one.

BOYO: What you got?

SID: You'll see now.

GWENNY: I know, *The Godfather*.

SID: How did you guess?

MOTHER: Who's the Godfather?

SID: Marlon Brando, Mam.

MOTHER: Oh… your father liked Marlon Brando.

BOYO: Film about the mafia.

MOTHER: The mafia?

SID: Yeah, you know, ice-cream sellers in Merthyr.

(*Laughter.*)

MOTHER: What are you laughing at?

GWENNY: Nothing, Mam, nothing.

SID: It's a good film, here it comes now, look.

GWENNY: You'll have to rewind it, Sid, it's in the middle.

MOTHER: Those boys don't come from Merthyr.

SID: I was joking.

GWENNY: They're Italian gangsters… hic… in America.

MOTHER: What they doing in America then?

BOYO: Don't wind her up, Sid.

GWENNY: There he is look.

MOTHER: Oh, Marlon Brando, he's put a lot of weight on.

BOYO: He can't act, mun, he's a mumbler.

MOTHER: We used to watch him when he was younger.

SID: He's no mumbler, Boyo, he's got style.

BOYO: What did he say then?

GWENNY: Something about Palermo.

MOTHER: Where's Palermo?

BOYO: Mumble, mumble, mumble.

SID: Can you remember some of his films, Mam?

MOTHER: No, but we watched them, let's see now.

GWENNY: *The Wild Ones*.

SID: That's not a Brando film.

MOTHER: Ugh, what have they put that horse's head in that man's bed for?

SID: It was his racehorse.

(BOYO *gets himself more drink.*)

GWENNY: You've got to know the story, Sid should rewind it back to the start.

SID: All right, hang on I'll rewind it.

MOTHER: Wasn't the film called *On The River* or something?

SID: *On The Waterfront*, that's what it was, great film.

BOYO: *On The Mumbles* it should have been.

GWENNY: Don't listen to him, he's being funny.

MOTHER: All the people in this film are going backwards.

BOYO: No wonder, they've got Marlon Brando in it.

SID: There, look, back to the start.

BOYO: 'Cos you can't have *On The Waterfront* without the Mumbles can you.

(BOYO *laughs out loud, and nearly falls over.*)

GWENNY: What's wrong with you, Boyo, be quiet and watch the film.

SID: Can't hold his booze, that what it is.

MOTHER: They've shot somebody now.

BOYO: Who wants to be a film star anyway?

GWENNY: Jealous he is.

BOYO: Pretending to be somebody else for a living, lies, all lies.

SID: Shut up, mun, and watch the film.

BOYO: It's a Mickey Mouse film.

SID: Any beer left in that, Gwenny?

MOTHER: Lot of killing going on, a musical I wanted.

(BOYO *starts to do a Brando impersonation.*)

MOTHER: What's Boyo doing?

GWENNY: Bad impressions of film stars.

SID: That one's called trying to be sober when you're pissed.

BOYO: What did I say then?

SID: Wasn't listening.

BOYO: You didn't understand me, did you?

GWENNY: You weren't doing it properly.

BOYO: Proves my point, he's a mumbler.

MOTHER: What did you say, Boyo?

BOYO: I said 'I could have been a contender, I could have been somebody.'

MOTHER: What did he say?

SID: He said it wrong, watch the film and he'll stop.

MOTHER: Not my kind of film.

SID: Oh Jesus.

GWENNY: Ssssh Sid.

BOYO: (*Shouting*) I said I could have been somebody, hear me. I could have been a boxer, or a farmer, or a miner, or I don't know, something real, something to get your teeth into, not lies, lies, actors, films fucking cloud cuckoo buckoo…

(*He stumbles and falls.* SID *turns the film off.*)

GWENNY: I was watching that.

SID: Forget it.

MOTHER: Not my cup of tea.

SID: There's something wrong with Boyo's head.

(SID *walks over to* BOYO *who's prostrate on the floor.*)

BOYO: What you do that for, you bastard?

MOTHER: Stop swearing, the two of you.

(SID *kicks* BOYO *when he's on the floor.* BOYO *retaliates and kicks back.*)

GWENNY: C'mon, the two of you, stop it. Like kids you are.

BOYO: He kicked me.

(SID *walks away and swigs a bottle.*)

MOTHER: I don't want any fighting in this house, got to stick together.

SID: Can't hold his beer that's all, alky he is.

BOYO: Who do you think you are then? Rambo? One hundred and eighty pints a night.

GWENNY: Stop it, the two of you, like kids.

MOTHER: Time for everybody to go to bed.

BOYO: Yeah… bed.

SID: You know what your problem is, Boyo, you don't know how to swing, you're stuck in a groove, mate.

BOYO: At least I'm not losing my hair and going old before my time.

(SID *throws a can at* BOYO.)

BOYO: Missed.

SID: Let's just wait and see who gets a job tomorrow, that's all I've got to say. That's depending on whether that car of yours can start.

BOYO: It'll start like a bird.

SID: Bet you we'll have to get a bus.

BOYO: I'm not getting involved in this crap.

MOTHER: Bed, boys and girl.

BOYO: Don't worry, I'm going.

SID: Goodnight, brother.

BOYO: Goodnight.

(BOYO *laughs and exits.*)

MOTHER: You two shouldn't argue.

SID: What did he want to buy a car with three wheels for, it's only three quarters of a car, typical of him, he's not all there.

GWENNY: C'mon Sid, give me a hand clearing up.

SID: How are you so sober then, Gwen?

GWENNY: Don't drink as much as you. You two shouldn't wind each other up.

SID: Him it is.

MOTHER: You should stick together.

SID: I mean fancy going 'On The Road' in Boyo's car – wouldn't get you as far as Swansea.

MOTHER: What you going on the road for, where you going?

GWENNY: If they get these jobs tomorrow, Mam, we'll all be able to go on the road – holiday somewhere.

MOTHER: I'd like that.

SID: Yeah, fly to America, hire a car, and drive right across it, chasing the sun.

MOTHER: America?

(GWENNY *makes eyes at* SID.)

SID: I've been reading this book, see, Mam, about these two blokes who drive across America, hitching, and mad they are, looking for a dream… Jack Kerouac his name is.

MOTHER: Oh…?

GWENNY: C'mon, Sid, help me clear up.

SID: We could do that, Mam, call in on Dad.

(*Pause.*)

SID: What you think? You've got his address and stuff.

(GWENNY *tips a bottle deliberately on the floor.*)

GWENNY: Oh… shit… you'll have to give me a hand, Sid.

MOTHER: I can't go, wouldn't be welcome, his floozy'll be there with him.

(GWENNY *forces* SID *to help her. They clear up.*)

MOTHER: (*She gets up.*) Goodnight all.

GWENNY: Goodnight, Mam.

SID: Goodnight.

(*She exits. There are sounds of industry and heavy machinery. Lights fade.*)

ACT TWO

(SID *and* BOYO *enter. They are on mountainside.*)

SID: That's it, Boyo, that is fucking it, that's the straw that bastard breaks the beaver's back.

BOYO: Don't let it get you down, wus.

SID: Get me down? I'm telling you I've played it by the book and it gets you nowhere, it's fucking typical.

BOYO: Could have got up earlier I suppose.

SID: Is that all you've got to say? Don't kid youself, Boyo, we could have queued up since last week, and I bet you they'd have found eight labourers to do the job before us. All over the country there's always eight labourers or eight shop assistants who get the job before you. They used to say I was too young, now we're too bastard old. That was the last chance I'm giving them to give me, Sid Lewis, a job. They've wrecked my plans and I've got to do something about it.

BOYO: They were Mickey Mouse jobs anyway, a dog could have done them.

SID: Anything with no brain and a coat could have

done them, that's the problem, Boyo, everything round here is Mickey Mouse, wus. Division four, small time, second class toys.

BOYO: The only way to look at it is to forget about it.

SID: I mean look at this, listen to this, 'No man shall operate any digging machinery of any kind without a labourer being present at all times.' In other words, you stand there like a lemon watching the machine. Bollocks – it's all bollocks.

BOYO: Sid, mun, I...

SID: I mean who wants to be a labourer for those shits? The least you can do is drive one of those machines. Imagine, there you are right, labouring in the middle of winter, tipping down with rain right, and you're in this black basin, haven't talked to a soul all day; so you look at the bloke in the machine and he's all snug and warm in his cab, and he calls you over, so you go over thinking he might want a chat and the crack. So you knock on his window and you ask him what he wants, and he turns round and says fuck off, I don't want to talk to you.

(BOYO *laughs*.)

BOYO: Remember when we were grave digging? The squally showers?

SID: Oh they were bastards. I tell you that's what's causing all the depression, that's what's affecting Mam's nerves.

BOYO: You never know where you stand, that's the worst with squally showers, like you never knew whether it was worth putting a coat on or not, like you're shovelling away, digging some poor bastard's grave in the rain and all of a sudden it stops, and you've got your coat on and you get too hot, so you take it off, the next thing you know it starts to rain again, so you put it back on again, and after a couple of days doing that you don't know if you've got your bastard coat on or off, so you're either boiling or wet, either way you can't make up your mind anyway, so you're a prime candidate for a cold, so you're off work, ending up hot, cold… confused.

SID: Depressed.

BOYO: Depressed… yeah…

SID: Poor.

BOYO: Yeah…coughing your lungs up, and you don't know who you are or whether you're coming or going, and you don't even know after all that who the hell's hole it is you're digging to bury him.

SID: Good job we're shot of that job, Boyo.

BOYO: And the labouring on the cast, it's the only way to look at it.

(*Pause.*)

SID: That money would have paid for a trip to America, Boyo.

BOYO: You wouldn't have gone anyway.

SID: How do you know?

BOYO: Because you're a fucking dreamer, that's why.

SID: No way, mate, I've been thinking about it, it's been in my head for ages, I'd be there, find out where the old man is, I'd be there. I was talking to Gwenny about it, she said she'd come too.

BOYO: Talked to her about it, have you?

SID: Yeah, and you know what?

BOYO: What?

SID: She's written the old man a few letters.

BOYO: How do you know?

SID: I was there when she wrote them.

BOYO: Where did she get the address then?

SID: She pestered Mam for it.

BOYO: He hasn't answered though, has he?

SID: No, but the main thing is she's got the address.

(*Pause.*)

SID: Plenty of work there too, Boyo, plenty of space, sun, sand, fancy riding across it chasing the sun on a Harley Davidson, money in your pocket, tiger in your tank, Hendrix on the Walkman – no helmet – just free and moving west.

BOYO: You can do that in Pembroke, Sid.

SID: Pembroke, don't give me Pembroke, what happens when you reach the sea, the end of the line?

BOYO: I don't know, you lie down on the beach and look at the sky.

SID: Watching the rain come down, no way, you wait for

low tide you do and ride hell for leather across the Atlantic.

BOYO: Can I ask you one question, Sid?

SID: Yeah, anything, say.

BOYO: Have you got a bike?

SID: Don't give me that shit now, will you?

BOYO: Well you haven't got a bike have you, and you're not far off thirty and you're skint.

SID: I don't want to know all right? All I know is that I wasn't born to live in this… in rain… it's not natural, I tell you I could live in a tent if the sun was shining.

BOYO: And you'd wake up in the morning singing Cat Stevens' songs – 'Morning has broken…'

SID: I tell you, I've been born in the wrong country, I have.

BOYO: You reckon, do you?

SID: Yeah, I reckon. If I had to answer a straight question, I'd have to say I wish I'd been born someone else, somewhere else.

BOYO: Oh yeah…like who?

SID: I don't know… someone else.

(*Pause.*)

Jack Kerouac.

BOYO: Never heard of him.

SID: He wrote this book I'm reading, *On The Road*.

BOYO: Are you telling me you want to write a book? You who hasn't read a book since he left school?

SID: No, mun, not write a book.

BOYO: What then?

SID: Have a life where something happens, like he went all round America, him and his mate, crazy bastards they were.

BOYO: Yeah?

SID: Yeah, I tell you something he said now, he said '… the only ones for me are the mad ones, mad to live, mad to talk, the ones who never yawn or say a commonplace thing, but burn, burn, burn, like fabulous yellow roman candles…' What you think of that, then?

BOYO: Yeah, it's good. American, was he?

SID: All his life.

BOYO: You don't have to go to America to find crazy bastards though, do you?

SID: He was looking for a dream, Boyo, chasing a dream.

BOYO: Did he find it?

SID: I don't know, I haven't finished the book yet – you can read it after me.

BOYO: Yeah, tell me when you've finished it.

SID: That's what the old man did, I reckon.

BOYO: What?

SID: Chased his dreams.

BOYO: Women he was after, Sid, not dreams.

SID: He saw his chance and woooofff he took it, can't blame him, can you?

BOYO: He was a bastard, Sid, he had responsibilities.

SID: Only half the size of his dreams, mate, that's the way I see it, fuckin' land of opportunity, innit? Nobody thought Tom Jones was a bastard and he went there.

BOYO: He did it 'cos of the tax, and anyway he's back now in the Vale.

SID: I thought you liked him, Boyo, just up your street, 'Green, green grass of home…' and that.

BOYO: Don't be so soft, will you.

SID: I've heard you playing his records, mate, him and Elvis.

BOYO: The Tom Jones is for Mam, Sid, the Elvis ones are mine. Elvis is the King, always was and always will be.

SID: That's it, see Boyo, that's what I'm talking about, he was the king, but look at Wales, where's its kings, where's our heroes? One answer, mate, we haven't got any. I mean let's face it, Boyo, Harry Secombe isn't a bloke I'd stand in the rain for, is he?

(BOYO *laughs*.)

Is he?

BOYO: You haven't half got a gob on you, Sid.

SID: It's called facing facts, wus, telling the truth about the way things are.

BOYO: Harry Secombe never said he was a hero.

SID: No, and he's fucking right too. No, I tell you, mate, I've had it up to here, from now on I'm going to do things my way.

BOYO: Your way?

SID: My way. The Sid Lewis experience.

(SID *and* BOYO *exit as Frank Sinatra's 'My Way' plays.*)

(*Lights up on Mam looking out of a window.* GWENNY *is looking at photographs.*)

MOTHER: Do you like Frank Sinatra, Gwenny?

GWENNY: Mmmm.

MOTHER: I'm glad you like him.

GWENNY: Why's that?

MOTHER: I'll be playing a lot of him from now on.

GWENNY: Will you?

MOTHER: Yes, to hide the noise from the open cast.

GWENNY: We can't only play Frank Sinatra, Mam, I've got records too.

MOTHER: I'll get to know them off by heart then.

(*Pause.*)

I'm glad the boys didn't get the jobs.

GWENNY: I'm not, we could have done with the money.

MOTHER: Money's not everything.

(*Beat.*)

MOTHER: Worrying about that and all this dreaming about America's making me ill.

GWENNY: Come and sit down here with me then.

(MOTHER *sits down and looks at the photos.*)

MOTHER: There's me and him there, look, on our honeymoon in Trafalgar Square, see all the pigeons.

GWENNY: He was handsome, wasn't he?

MOTHER: I'm telling you, like Errol Flynn, but here, look, wait till you see this photo.

GWENNY: Ahhh… what's that in his hair?

MOTHER: Pigeon shit, he went to stand by the fountain and a pigeon did a mess in his hair.

(GWENNY *laughs.*)

I thought it was funny too, but he didn't like it, he was tampin' it, he wanted to go and clean it off, but I said it was bad luck, but he wouldn't listen. He went to the gents and cleaned it off, he wouldn't listen.

GWENNY: Spoilsport wasn't he?

MOTHER: He was happy then, liked to wander he did, real wanderer.

GWENNY: What year was it?

MOTHER: Nineteen fifty-seven.

GWENNY: Was it? There's a coincidence now.

MOTHER: What is?

GWENNY: Same year Joyce Johnson met Jack Kerouac, January, 1957.

MOTHER: This was in May, spring wedding.

GWENNY: Same year though, Mam.

MOTHER: Who are they then, I don't know them, do I?

GWENNY: I'm reading a book about them, Sid lent it to me, it's a love story.

MOTHER: They're not from round here, then?

GWENNY: No, this was in New York, it's a lovely sad, happy story so far.

MOTHER: What's that got to do with my wedding then?

GWENNY: Well, nothing, I suppose, just a coincidence.

(*Sound of someone approaching.* SID *and* BOYO *enter.*)

BOYO: Well, we've got enough wood for ten years.

MOTHER: Good news, keep the fire burning.

SID: No wood left on the trees anywhere in the country if we carry on like this.

MOTHER: Musn't forget the fire.

GWENNY: Hey, Boyo, come and have a look at these photos.

BOYO: Oh Christ, look at the state of me.

SID: Cool shades, Boyo, I don't remember you being such a cool kid.

BOYO: Stick insect, that's what I was.

MOTHER: Wouldn't eat his food.

SID: What about Gwenny here then with no front teeth?

(*Laughter.*)

GWENNY: Look at Sid here pulling a jib.

SID: I couldn't swim that's why, and all you buggers were swimming.

GWENNY: What's this one here?

MOTHER: Your father giving the three of you a bath.

SID: Gwenny was only about six, look, and even then she's got two boys in the bath with her.

(GWENNY *playfully pushes* SID. *Laughter.* MOTHER *switches on the TV. It's off channel.*)

BOYO: Has the telly broken down then?

MOTHER: No.

BOYO: The reception's bad, innit?

MOTHER: It's all right for me.

BOYO: There's no picture on it.

MOTHER: I've seen enough pictures for one night.

BOYO: Let me adjust it.

MOTHER: No.

BOYO: It's getting on my nerves, you can't sit there and watch something like that.

MOTHER: I said no, leave it alone.

(BOYO *can only give her an exasperated look.*)

SID: 'Home in Missoula, home in truckee, home in Poelousas ain't no home for me...'

GWENNY: Home in old Medora...

SID: Home in Wounded Knee...

GWENNY: Home in... what is it?

SID: Ogallalla.

GWENNY: That's it.

SID: Home I'll never be.

(*Laughter.*)

That's my Joycey.

BOYO: What did you say?

MOTHER: He called her Joyce.

(*Laughter.*)

BOYO: Cmon, mun, what's the joke, who's Joyce?

GWENNY: Joyce Johnson, Jack Kerouac's girlfriend, you know.

BOYO: No.

GWENNY: She was his girlfriend.

(SID *puts his arm around* GWENNY *playfully.*)

They sang that song together.

BOYO: Yeah?

SID: Yeah, good song.

GWENNY: From this book, Boyo.

(*She shows him* On The Road.)

BOYO: What's so special about that, then?

(MOTHER *turns the volume up on the TV.* SID *shouts over it, making a point.*)

SID: It's more than a book, brother, it's a way of life.

GWENNY: Mam, turn it down a bit, we can't hear.

(*Starts reading from the book.*)

'I got on the Washington bus, wasted some time there wandering around, went out of my way to see the Blue Ridge, heard the bird of Shenandoah and visited Stonewall Jackson's grave; at dusk stood in the Kanawha river, the dark and mysterious Ohio and Cincinnati at dawn then Indiana fields again, and at St. Louis…'

(MOTHER *suddenly gets up from the chair, walks towards* SID *and spanks him.*)

SID: What the...

(*Laughter.*)

BOYO: Hey mun, Mam, c'mon.

MOTHER: Don't laugh at your brother, they were laughing at you, can't you hear them?

BOYO: Just forget it.

SID: Don't ever do that again, Mam.

GWENNY: There wasn't any need to do that.

MOTHER: You were laughing.

SID: So what, is there a law against laughing here?

BOYO: Come and sit down here.

SID: What the hell's wrong with her? We were only having a sing song and a read, I tell you that was out of order.

GWENNY: Forget it, she didn't mean it.

(BOYO *turns off the set.*)

MOTHER: I was listening to that.

(*She switches it back on.*)

GWENNY: Turn it off, Mam, please.

MOTHER: No, it's the only company I've got here... me and Mr Snow. Some people call him interference, but he's Mr Snow, we get on like a house on fire. I get up in the morning and say hello to Mr Snow, and then before he's got time to answer I turn him off.

(*He switches it off. Silence.*)

He's the only friend I've got in this house. He was born when the crane blocked the signal. Hey, you're not listening to me.

SID: You're rambling again.

MOTHER: That's what you call it, is it? I tell you, I've told Mr Snow everything, all my secrets... he's good like that, I've told him everything I can't tell my own kids... keeps me company, and we all need company. You listening, Sid Lewis? Gwenny? You understand what I'm saying, all the secrets, but there's nothing funny going on between us… not like some things I see, he knows more about this house than you do, Boyo, like I wouldn't like to say there's anything funny going on between Sid and Gwenny, I mean they're brother and sister, but Joyce and Jack, they're different.

SID: What are you trying to say?

MOTHER: They were lovers, see Boyo, Jack and Joyce… in love, that's all I'm saying.

GWENNY: I never thought you'd ever say something like that, Mam. I never thought there'd come a day.

BOYO: C'mon, Mam, you don't know what you're saying now.

MOTHER: Oh yes I do.

SID: I'm not listening to this crap any more, I'm off.

MOTHER: Don't bother, Sid… what you looking at me like that for – all of you, can't wait to get me out of the house, well don't worry, I'm going, I'm going to pack.

BOYO: Pack?

GWENNY: Where do you think you're going to go?

MOTHER: Haven't thought about it, but it's getting too hot for me in this house I can tell you.

BOYO: Hey, Mam, Sid knows you didn't mean it, don't you, Sid?

SID: Yeah…

MOTHER: Oh, I do though, and I'll do it again.

SID: You're not going to do it again, don't worry.

MOTHER: Not safe for me in this house any more. I know you want me out of the house. Somebody's been painting my room blue.

SID: Here we go again.

GWENNY: We've told you, Mam, it's always been blue.

MOTHER: Painting my room that colour's the last straw. I know the truth, I can't... I can't...

(*She breaks down.* GWENNY *tries to comfort her.*)

GWENNY: C'mon, Mam, I'll make some tea.

MOTHER: I'm going, I'm going.

(GWENNY *leads her away. They exit.*)

SID: Phone the doctor, she's got to see a doctor, Boyo.

BOYO: No. He'll say she'll have to go in the mental to recover, nervous breakdown it is, and she doesn't want to go out of the house, you know how she is.

SID: We can't help her, Boyo, she's getting worse, I tell you she needs a doctor and I'm going to phone him.

(*Pause.*)

BOYO: I suppose we'll have to, but she's not going unless she definitely has to.

(SID *exits.* BOYO *looks around resignedly. Lights fade to blackout.*)

(*Fade in loud opera music, Maria Callas singing an aria perhaps, as the red light of a fire builds, revealing* MOTHER *burning clothes.* BOYO *enters in his pants, half asleep.*)

BOYO: What you burning, Mam?

MOTHER: Oh, Boyo, nothing, just seeing to the fire.

BOYO: You know what time it is?

MOTHER: No, I was too busy.

BOYO: Come away from the fire. You trying to burn us to death or what?

(SID *enters, also in his pants.*)

SID: There's nothing on the walls, Mam, only paint. Oh Boyo, you heard the commotion as well, did you?

BOYO: What's going on then?

MOTHER: Just burning some old clothes, your father's clothes, see?

BOYO: Oh, Christ, they're my clothes, mun, what the hell mun, Mam, give them here.

SID: Thought I recognised them. (*Laughs.*)

BOYO: Don't laugh, mun.

SID: Mam's been doing a bit of painting, see, Boyo, red. She's got paint everywhere.

BOYO: Half my clothes are in the fire.

MOTHER: I've got paint on my clothes too.

SID: I can tell you why she's been doing it too.

MOTHER: I couldn't help it.

SID: It's all right… ssshhh…

BOYO: Why, Mam?

SID: She says there was blood on the walls.

MOTHER: Not thinks, knows. I couldn't get it off. It was getting on my nerves.

SID: She says it's Dad's blood.

MOTHER: It is his blood, the cat's out of the bag now.

SID: I don't know any more, that's all she told me.

MOTHER: They're going to take me away, Boyo, but you said no matter what I'd done you'd always love me, and if something happens to me you've got to stick together, you hear me?

BOYO: All right, Mam, it's all right. How about getting you back to bed now though, uh?

MOTHER: No, not in there.

SID: How did the blood get there then, Mam?

MOTHER: Because I killed him.

(*Silence.* MOTHER *begins to laugh hysterically.* SID *and* BOYO *watch mesmerised. She eventually stops. Silence.*)

MOTHER: The cat… is… out… of the bag.

BOYO: All right, Mam, it's all right.

(*Silence.*)

MOTHER: What have I said?

SID: You said you felt like sleeping.

MOTHER: Did I? I do too.

BOYO: Are you ready to go to bed, Mam?

MOTHER: Yes, I'm tired now, bed is best.

SID: C'mon, I'll give you a hand.

MOTHER: No, no, I can manage on my own, but I'll go to your room, my room gives me nightmares.

BOYO: You sure you can go on your own?

MOTHER: Course I can, I'm not old, and I'm still your Mother.

(*They watch her as she exits.*)

BOYO: Fucking hell.

SID: Had a nightmare she has, that's all. Her mind playing tricks with her.

BOYO: Is that what you think?

SID: Course it is, you don't believe her, do you?

BOYO: I don't know what to believe, Sid.

SID: Everybody knows he's in America, you ask anybody. She never killed him, she probably wishes she did, and now that she's ill she thinks she has done, got it all mixed up in her head, that's all.

BOYO: I tell you, I don't know whether I'm coming or going, too much for me this is.

SID: Don't let it get to you, brother, it's all in her mind, believe me, she's telling lies, it's in her head.

BOYO: How come we haven't heard a word from him since he went then?

SID: Because he probably thinks it's the only way. I bet you he's laying plans now for us to go over there on a visit. That's my opinion anyway.

BOYO: How can you be that sure, Sid?

SID: I know, mun, I've got a feeling about it, I believe that's all, if I didn't look at it that way I'd go nuts.

(*Pause.*)

BOYO: No point in saying anything to Gwenny.

SID: No it'll make her worry, confuse her, best thing to do is forget about it, and hope she gets better. Goodnight, I'm off to bed.

BOYO: Goodnight.

(SID *exits.* BOYO *stands, looks through photo album. Music plays softly to blackout.*)

ACT THREE

(*'Riders On The Storm' plays in blackout. Lights up on* SID *doing well with the card trick on the table.* BOYO *doing press-ups on the floor. Music fades out.*)

SID: Oi... Boyo, what you reckon to this masterpiece then?

BOYO: That's all right innit, how did you get that far then?

SID: Solid foundation, Boyo. Everything Sid Lewis builds is solid. Skill too – two of them together, fatal combination, mate.

BOYO: No flies on you see, are there, brother?

SID: No, and the odd ones I do find flying around my head either went to Oxford or Cambridge.

BOYO: On a day trip.

SID: No, Boyo, only because of their brains, Boyo, only 'cos of their brains.

(GWENNY *enters.*)

GWENNY: Never guess what I've just seen.

(GWENNY *stands still in the middle of the room.*)

I was walking down the street right, and it's raining, the clouds were low, and in front of me is someone walking a dog, it's a chihuahua.

(*Pause.*)

Then I hear this bus coming down the road behind me, a big red bus like a school bus, and it passes me, whoosh, like that, and it's just about to pass the dog, who's on a lead, when the dog strays into the road, and gets squashed flat, and the owner's still holding onto the lead, just staring at the squashed dog. And all of a sudden I feel like laughing, not just a giggle, but a hysterical one.

(*Pause.*)

SID: Yeah, what it is right, is that somewhere deep down inside, you just hate chihuahuas.

GWENNY: Why? Then I go and see if I can help. The man's just staring down, I feel sorry for him now. Then he turns around and says 'I've only just given him a whole tin of chum, and now the poor bugger's gone and got squashed'. Then I asked him what the dog's name was and he turns round and says 'Jack'.

SID: Kerouac.

GWENNY: That's what I said, and he says, 'Who's that?' and I says 'He's an American who wrote books.' So the two of us stand there, looking at this American novelist who's squashed on the road, and you know what?

SID: What?

GWENNY: I haven't thought of an ending to it yet.

(*She squeals in victory.*)

BOYO: Oh, Christ mun, Gwenny.

SID: Hey come on, Gwenny, give us the ending, got to be an ending.

GWENNY: And the girl turned to her brother and said I made it all up. I was dreaming. I've never even seen a chihuahua, and what's more, I haven't been out of the house either. I've been in my room reading, and trying on clothes.

(*She looks at them and they all laugh, Sudden loud crash of industry offstage.*)

BOYO: Jesus, are they blowing up the world or what?

(*Goes to the window.*)

SID: Fuck 'em. I've got a masterpiece going here. Hey, seen my cards, Gwenny?

BOYO: You can see the top of the cranes now, look.

GWENNY: They'll eat the house one day.

SID: Let's go up and have a look.

GWENNY: What now?

SID: Yeah, come on.

GWENNY: You coming, Boyo?

BOYO: No, I'll stay here and guard the house.

SID: Come on then…

(SID *gets up and accidentally tumbles the cards. We see that* SID *has glued his card trick together.*)

Shit.

BOYO: Ah… look, Gwenny, look. That's why his card trick works… he's glued them all together! (*Holding up the card trick.*)

GWENNY: That's cheating, Sid.

BOYO: Yeah…

SID: Well it just goes to show, see brother, don't believe all you see.

BOYO: Yeah, I'll remember that.

SID: C'mon, Gwenny, let's go.

(SID *and* GWENNY *exit.*)

(*Lights change and come up on the open cast mine. A labourer appears with a shovel.* SID *and* GWENNY *enter.*)

SID: See that bloke over there, Gwenny?

GWENNY: Yeah.

SID: He's a labourer, he got the job me and Boyo should have had.

GWENNY: Looks as if he's lost something.

(*They walk towards the labourer who's staring at the floor and leaning on his shovel.*)

SID: All right?

LAB: Do you work here?

SID: No, we live in the house down there.

GWENNY: All the blasting is affecting our house, every blast shakes it.

LAB: Nothing to do with me, go and tell the gaffer.

SID: Where's he?

LAB: In the shed on the top there, but I wouldn't bother.

SID: Why not?

LAB: He's dead.

GWENNY: Uh?

LAB: Dead he is, you got time for a chat?

SID: Yeah, but…

LAB: Don't worry about him, they give him bacon sandwiches and he's right, don't have a chance to talk here see.

GWENNY: What you looking for then?

LAB: I'm not looking for nothing, given up that crack.

SID: What's on the floor then?

LAB: I've lost something.

SID: What have you lost?

(LABOURER *looks at him.*)

LAB: What kind of question's that, wus?

SID: We saw you looking at the floor. You said you've lost something.

GWENNY: We'll help you find it.

LAB: I don't want to find it, it'll upset me. I've lost it I know, but that doesn't mean I want to find it, does it?

And you can't find something you're not looking for.

SID: I tried for this job see, me and my brother. I…

LAB: Here, you can have a go if you want.

SID: What you have to do?

LAB: Nothing or everything, does your head in.

GWENNY: How do you mean?

LAB: We're standing on coal, innit? That machine over there is, and that lorry is. The machine fills the lorry with coal, and my job is to throw the bits of coal that tip over back on the lorry, you got me? But the trick is, how can you tell which bits fell off the lorry, 'cos it all looks the same, don't it? So you either shovel everything you see back in the lorry, or you don't bother.

SID: And you don't bother.

LAB: No, my head's gone. Hey mind your heads, the driver's stoned out of his box. The bloke before him got sacked because he wouldn't get out of his cab. He tried to drive it home, by the time he'd got there it was time to come back to work, so he's forgotten where he lives now.

GWENNY: They look like dinosaurs.

LAB: No, the dinosaur's extinct.

GWENNY: Electric dinosaurs.

LAB: If you want, yeah.

SID: Do you talk to the bloke in the cab?

LAB: Sometimes he tells me to go to the store for a long wait, so I go, and wait there all day. Best part of the job.

GWENNY: Lucky you didn't get the jobs, Sid.

(SID *nods.*)

SID: What is it you've lost then?

LAB: My head.

(GWENNY *laughs.*)

Is it funny? (*Suddenly aggressive.*)

GWENNY: No, no, it's just me, laughing.

SID: How did it happen?

LAB: Things weren't going my way when I was younger. I was about eighteen and I put my head in the sand. I took it out when they gave me this job, but when I looked in the mirror, I didn't recognize the face looking back at me. This new face was different to the one I put in the sand.

SID: How do you mean?

LAB: Well, the old face for a start was younger, but that's nothing, the old face had clear eyes, the mouth used to laugh and talk about plans for the rest of the body, and the brain used to dream a lot, you follow me?

SID: What's wrong with the new face?

LAB: The new face is different, the eyes have lost their shine, the skin is sagging, the teeth are rotting, the hair is turning grey, the plans have got dust on them, and the dreams have just fallen out of the ears, can you see? That's why I reckon I must have lost it, came off when I wasn't looking, and all those things happened because it's been kicked about on the floor, like lorries gone over it.

GWENNY: Dinosaurs eaten it.

LAB: Yeah, sheep pissed on it, slug trails all over the brain and cobwebs in the memory.

SID: Hey listen, mate, you've got to find it, I'll give you a hand.

LAB: Is there something wrong with you?

GWENNY: He wants to help.

LAB: That head's lost for good, this is the one I'm stuck with now. I just wish I hadn't put it in the sand in the first place, I might not have lost it, 'cos I know in my bones I've lost something, gives me an ache in my guts. I don't want to find it now, it's too late, it's too fucking late.

(*Pause.*)

SID: That won't happen to me.

LAB: You reckon?

SID: Yeah, I'm off I am.

LAB: Where you going?

SID: Going to America we are, me and my sister here.

LAB: I've got to go now, see the machine's started walking, got to follow the machine.

GWENNY: We'll come again if you want.

LAB: Yeah, come if you want.

GWENNY: What's you name?

LAB: Oh, I don't know, make one up.

GWENNY: You've got to have a name,

LAB: Clint.

GWENNY: My name's Gwenny, and this is my brother, Si...

SID: Jack.

(GWENNY *looks at him.*)

Jack Kerouac.

LAB: Clint Eastwood, I'm the man with no name.

(LABOURER *laughs and walks away.*)

GWENNY: What did you want to say that for?

SID: I don't know, for a laugh.

GWENNY: I'm not coming up here again, something crazy about it.

SID: I know what he's saying though, do you?

(GWENNY *nods.*)

GWENNY: C'mon, I want to go.

SID: You go, I'll follow you down now.

(GWENNY *exits.* SID *is looking out. Sound of industry increases. Sound of wind and screaming.*)

SID: Sid Lewis R.I.P.

(SID *walks away.*)

(*Lights up on* MOTHER *in a hospital room.* BOYO *enters.*)

BOYO: Hello, Mam?

MOTHER: Yes Jesus, it's me, Mrs Lewis.

BOYO: No, Mam, it's me, Boyo.

(MOTHER *looks around*.)

MOTHER: Oh, I thought you were Jesus.

(*Pause*.)

BOYO: I brought you some fruit.

MOTHER: Oh, put them over there.

(BOYO *puts the fruit down*.)

BOYO: Not a bad room, Mam.

MOTHER: What do you want here?

BOYO: Came to see you that's all.

MOTHER: How's the house?

BOYO: All right.

(*Pause*.)

BOYO: Gwenny keeps writing him letters to America.

MOTHER: You'll have to tell her to stop.

BOYO: I've been reading them.

MOTHER: I've told you already, he's not there.

BOYO: I don't want to upset her. They're calling her Miss America.

MOTHER: Who is?

BOYO: The Post Office. The woman told me she comes in

every week to see if there's a letter.

MOTHER: What fruit did you bring?

BOYO: Apples, do you want one?

(MOTHER *takes an apple*.)

Did you give her an address, Mam?

MOTHER: I can't remember.

BOYO: Sid told me you gave it to her.

MOTHER: She was pestering me.

BOYO: So you did then?

MOTHER: Yes.

BOYO: So he is in America?

MOTHER: An address doesn't mean anything.

BOYO: What's the address then?

(*Silence.*)

Mam?

MOTHER: Mr Clem Lewis, Main Street, Dodge City, The West, America.

(*She laughs.*)

BOYO: Is that what you've given Gwenny?

(*Laughter.*)

Is it?

(MOTHER *laughs*.)

BOYO: She must know it's wrong, she can't believe that.

MOTHER: You better ask her, she's the one sending the letters. Me and Mr Snow were sitting there one day and there was a Western on, and I turned round to Gwenny and said that's where he'll be. But you know what the worst of it is, he didn't have to bother to think of going to America, and you tell Sid and Gwenny not to waste their money. Somebody in here told me you don't have to go to the Wild West to find America, they've built a Wild West up in the valley – you can go there and be a cowboy for a day. You can dress in your cowboy outfit, have a drink in the saloon, and they've got Country and Western singers every Friday and Saturday night. If your father had only waited a bit, he'd still be here. The bloke who told me is a cowboy, he thinks he's a cowboy anyway.

(*She laughs. Pause.*)

BOYO: I'm going now, Mam.

MOTHER: To guard the house. I think I'm lucky to be in here, nobody'll hurt me in here. I hear you can see the open cast from the window now.

(BOYO *nods.*)

MOTHER: They're coming nearer, won't be long now.

BOYO: I love Gwenny, Mam, and I don't want to lie to her.

MOTHER: Tell her the truth.

BOYO: I don't know what it is.

MOTHER: You still don't believe me, do you?

(*Lights change. Fade up on Lou Reed's 'Walk On The Wild Side'.*

SID *is reading to* GWENNY, BOYO *sits at the table, annoyed.*)

SID: 'I'm with you in Rockland, where we hug and kiss the United States under our bedsheets, the United States that coughs all night and won't let us sleep.'

(*Pause.*)

'Where we wake up electrified out of the coma by our own souls, airplanes roaring over the roof, they've come to drop angelic bombs, the hospital illuminates itself, imaginary walls collapse, victory, forget you're underwater, we're free in my dreams, you walk dripping from a sea journey on the highway across America in tears to the door of my cottage in the Western night.'

BOYO: What in fuck's name are you talking about, Sid?

SID: Freedom, brother, escape.

GWENNY: Do you think Joyce Johnson's pretty, Sid?

(*During the following dialogue* BOYO *finds a bottle of pills on the table which* GWENNY *nonchalantly takes away from him.*)

SID: Yeah.

GWENNY: She wore nice clothes, nobody I know dresses like that.

SID: Fifties see.

GWENNY: Where's the Upper West Side?

SID: New York.

GWENNY: Greenwich Village?

SID: That's where she met Jack.

BOYO: You finished that book then?

SID: Yeah, ages ago, Gwenny's read it too, do you want to borrow it?

BOYO: No, I'm all right.

GWENNY: 'Putting on a pair of copper earrings en route to Jack…'

(GWENNY *looks in the mirror, puts on earrings.*)

Do you like these, Sid?

(SID *nods.*)

SID: You could look as pretty as her, Gwen.

GWENNY: Think so?

SID: No trouble.

GWENNY: Even without the copper earrings?

SID: They don't have to be copper, just big and round.

GWENNY: And then a black skirt, jumper.

SID: And black stockings. I could call you Joyce.

GWENNY: And then all you need is a pair of faded old jeans and like a lumberjack shirt and I could call you Jack.

SID: You could be my girlfriend.

GWENNY: And Boyo, you can be Allen Ginsberg or somebody.

BOYO: It's all right. I'll stick to being Boyo.

(GWENNY *pulls a face at him behind his back.*)

SID: It was him that introduced Jack to Joyce.

BOYO: Oh great, mun.

GWENNY: It was a love story see, Boyo.

BOYO: How long am I going to have to listen to this crap?

GWENNY: Don't be like that.

BOYO: Well Christ, mun, it's the same old crack every day, Jack this, Joyce that, why don't you give it a rest.

SID: Read the book, then you can join in.

BOYO: I don't want to read the book, I'm not interested, you're like a pair of kids, mun, playing.

GWENNY: Nothing wrong with that, is there?

BOYO: I'm not saying that but it's all this yankage, give it a rest for Christ sake.

GWENNY: Oh, poor Boyo, he feels left out, Jack.

(*She smooths his hair.*)

BOYO: Get off mun, Gwenny.

SID: Stop feeling sorry for yourself, Boyo.

BOYO: I'm not, but I'm sick to death with all this fucking dreaming about America. If you don't like it here, why don't you just fuck off out of here on the first plane?

SID: If I had the money, Boyo, I'd be long gone.

BOYO: The sooner the better, and you're just as bad Gwen, all these letters.

GWENNY: How do you know I've been writing letters?

BOYO: Mam told me, and she showed me his address too.

GWENNY: So.

BOYO: Well, it's false, innit? She made it up.

GWENNY: How do you know?

BOYO: Well it's obvious, innit? There's no number or nothing, and she got it out of a Western – Dodge City, The West.

GWENNY: I don't care, he'll get it somehow.

BOYO: Don't be so soft, mun, there's millions of Lewis's in America.

GWENNY: I don't care what you say, it won't stop me, and at least we'll have somewhere to go when the open cast takes over the house.

BOYO: It's not going to take over the house.

SID: Course it is, it's coming nearer every day, before long they'll be knocking on the door saying 'Oi, we want your house' and you'll say, 'You can't have it, it's part of a street', and they'll turn around and say, 'We know, but we own the street', and then where will you be?

GWENNY: Everybody'll go in the end Boyo, there's nothing here for us any more, it's a forgotten town. You've got to think ahead, keep your options open.

BOYO: Think it's as easy as that do you? Just clear off. Well, I don't know about you, but this is where I belong and I'm staying, no fucking tinpot dreaming for me.

SID: You know what's wrong with you, you've got your

head in the sand, and I know what happens to people like that.

BOYO: Mam told us we had to stick together, and she's right.

SID: Mam's lost her marbles, or haven't you noticed?

(BOYO *runs at* SID. *A stand off.*)

Got to change and swing with the crack, and I'm making plans for it. The only ones for me are the ones who burn, got me, Boyo?

BOYO: Like a planet is it, Gwenny?

(BOYO *looks disgusted. Lights change.* SID *and* GWENNY *drink bourbon and swallow pills as Lou Reed's* New York *album plays.*)

SID: Girl met boy on a blind date arranged by Allen Ginsberg, it was January 1957.

GWENNY: The girl was Joyce Johnson.

SID: The boy was Jack Kerouac.

GWENNY: You can be Allen Grinsberg, Boyo.

(BOYO *enters.*)

BOYO: What you playing?

GWENNY: Playing out a love story.

BOYO: Who the hell is Allen Ginsberg?

SID: He's a poet.

GWENNY: He introduced two lovers.

BOYO: This is Jack, and this is Joyce, how's that?

SID: Help yourself to the Jack Daniels, Joyce.

BOYO: And don't tell me he's a baseball player.

SID: Wrong – it's a whisky.

BOYO: Well, Jack, did you find your American dream?

GWENNY: That's not a fair question, Boyo.

BOYO: Why not?

SID: No, I went half mad in 1967, and died in my Mother's arms.

BOYO: Not much of a dream then is it?

GWENNY: If you're not going to play the game properly, there's no point in playing.

BOYO: Forget your bastard games, I'm going down the pub to get pissed.

(*He exits.*)

SID: Care for a dance, Joyce?

GWENNY: Sure, Jack.

(*Presley's 'Love Me Tender' comes on, and there is something strangely sexual about the dance. While this goes on BOYO knocks back the booze, in another part of the stage. The dance comes to an end, and BOYO staggers in, drunk. GWENNY is leaning on SID's shoulder, music low in background.*)

BOYO: The lovers still on their feet, and I've got a poem for them, a Boyo poem, want to hear it? Any minute now, a cup of tea is going to come in here, sit down, watch me light a cigarette, and as the smoke and steam rise it's going to get slowly, contentedly… drunk.

(BOYO *tries to join in, and the atmosphere changes.*)

GWENNY: Get off, Boyo, will you, spoilt it all now.

(GWENNY *walks away.*)

BOYO: Hey, where you going, come back I haven't finished yet, we've…

(GWENNY *exits.*)

SID: Sit down, before you fall down, shit for brains.

BOYO: Got to stick together, mun, oi, don't go to bed now mun, I'm a bit pissed, that's all.

SID: Thanks, mate, thanks a lot.

BOYO: Cat and the boys were asking after you, Sid…. If you can't bring… hic… Mohammed to the mountain, take the mountain to him… or something.

(SID *exits.*)

I drink coke, eat popcorn, wear baseball hats, watch the films, but all I'm asking what…who the fuck is Jack Kerouac, and these books? A book is a book, Bill and Ben the flower pot men, I remember that book… stay and have a drink with your brother… I've got the cans, got the chips. Have a chip, have a kip – it's a poem, Allen Ginsberg, eat your heart out, pal.

(*Falls over.*)

I'm confused I am, always confusion, messy…somebody turn the light out.

(*Blackout. Discordant music plays. Lights up on* MOTHER, *wearing a Welsh hat and daffodil.* BOYO *is dreaming.*)

MOTHER: Boyo! Sid? Gwenny?

(*Silence.*)

BOYO: Where's the wind coming from?

(*Silence.*)

Sid? Gwenny?

MOTHER: It's not Gwenny, it's me.

BOYO: Mam, what the hell are you doing here?

MOTHER: I live here.

BOYO: How did you get out of the hospital?

MOTHER: This is the hospital.

BOYO: What you got that hat on for?

MOTHER: It's only a hat, did you think I'd walk in here with no hat on or what?

BOYO: I'll have to take you back to the hospital now.

MOTHER: Don't talk rubbish, this is the hospital.

(BOYO *looks at her.*)

BOYO: Christ, it's freezing in here.

MOTHER: You let the fire go out, that's why.

BOYO: It wasn't my fault, I've been out all night. Gwenny was here, she should have been looking after the fire.

MOTHER: You like your drink, don't you?

BOYO: I'm not going to argue, Mam. I'll go and get Gwenny.

MOTHER: What you mean, go and get Gwenny?

BOYO: She's upstairs, sleeping.

MOTHER: There's no upstairs here.

(BOYO *stares at her.*)

You go and have a look.

(BOYO *picks up the candle and wanders around.*)

BOYO: What the hell's this, where the hell am I?

MOTHER: In the hospital, where do you think you are?

BOYO: I must have fallen asleep in the house, how the hell did I get here and where's Gwenny… and Sid?

MOTHER: Gone.

BOYO: What do you mean, Mam, gone, what gone?

MOTHER: Gone away.

(MOTHER *exits.* BOYO *runs around shouting and screaming, cacophony of discordant noise and percussion. He collapses. Blackout. Then* GWENNY *appears in her dressing gown. Lights up.*)

GWENNY: Boyo, wake up.

(GWENNY *shakes him gently and he wearily opens his eyes. On seeing her he shoots back in reaction.*)

BOYO: Get away from me, get away from me.

GWENNY: Sssh… Boyo, it's all right, it's me.

(BOYO *stares hard at her and looks around, slowly getting his bearings.*)

GWENNY: You must have had a nightmare, you've been ranting and raving. You woke me up.

(*He continues to stare at her.*)

GWENNY: It's all right now.

BOYO: What time is it?

GWENNY: Time to go to bed, it's late.

BOYO: Where's everybody gone? Mam was here and Sid.

GWENNY: All in bed, that's where you should be.

(BOYO *holds his head in his hands.*)

GWENNY: You drank too much. All right now?

BOYO: My head's like a bucket. (*Nods.*) It's all right now, you go to bed.

(GWENNY *looks at him.*)

GWENNY: See you tomorrow.

BOYO: Gwenny.

GWENNY: What?

BOYO: Where's Sid?

GWENNY: Sleeping, where do you think he is?

(GWENNY *exits.* BOYO *lights a cigarette and thinks. Lights change. Exterior house.* SID *is chopping wood with an axe.* BOYO *is sick in a corner.*)

SID: How's your head?

BOYO: Coming off, and my mouth's as dry as an Arab's dap.

SID: What time did you get to bed in the end?

BOYO: I don't know – late.

SID: See anybody you knew in the pub?

BOYO: A few, they were asking after you.

(*Pause.*)

Where did you sleep last night?

SID: In the bed, where do you think I slept?

BOYO: You weren't in there this morning when I looked in.

SID: ==I was in Gwenny's bed that's why. She got a bit tight last night as well.== I had to carry her to bed, she fell asleep down here, and I took her up, and I fell asleep there too.

BOYO: Looked all right to me, she heard me, I was having bad dreams, she came to see if I was all right.

SID: What you trying to say?

BOYO: I wanted to know.

SID: Yeah, but I can see what you're thinking, and I don't like it.

BOYO: When I saw you last night, dancing – I don't know, it didn't look right.

SID: Gwenny's my sister for fuck sake.

BOYO: I saw the way you were looking at her.

SID: You'd better watch what you're saying, mate.

(*Facing up to* BOYO.)

BOYO: Lay off, Sid, I was only asking.

SID: You better take a good look at youself, saying things like that.

BOYO: It was all the Jack and Joyce stuff.

SID: That was a game, Boyo, playing a game.

BOYO: It didn't look like a game to me, that's what I'm saying.

SID: Well you're wrong, you're talking incest for Christ's sake.

(*Pause.*)

BOYO: Hey, Sid, forget I said it, I'm sorry, didn't mean that.

SID: Good job you didn't tell Gwenny.

BOYO: Yeah, yeah, look I said I'm sorry, we're living on top of each other, it's getting to me that's all.

SID: We'll just forget about it, O.K?

BOYO: Yeah, sorry.

(SID *continues to chop wood.*)

SID: I tell you what you need, Boyo, is a girlfriend, help take your mind off things.

BOYO: What about you then?

SID: Do me good too I know, but I'm not the marrying kind, see Boyo – fucking minefield if you ask me, anyway you're the one that's staying, I'll be off. But if you do get married when I'm gone and you have a Kevin or a Helen you make sure they don't grow up to pull the wings off butterflies and throw fireworks at the old age. I'll see you back in the house.

BOYO: Hey, I thought I'd call in on Mam, you coming?

SID: No, I'll see you back at the house.

(SID *exits. Lights change. Come up on* MOTHER *in the hospital wearing a Welsh hat and daffodil.* BOYO *enters looking dishevelled and confused.*)

MOTHER: What are you looking at me like that for?

BOYO: Why you wearing those clothes?

MOTHER: You don't know then?

BOYO: Know what?

MOTHER: You've forgotten.

BOYO: Forgotten what?

MOTHER: Tell me what the date is?

BOYO: I don't know, end of February.

MOTHER: Wrong, it's March the 1st, it's St. David's Day and you've forgotten.

BOYO: And that's why you're wearing your clothes.

MOTHER: Some of us don't forget.

BOYO: I lost touch of the days, and I had this dream and you were wearing those clothes.

MOTHER: I don't want to hear your excuses.

(*Pause.*)

Like my daffodil?

BOYO: It's plastic.

MOTHER: Didn't have real ones, and the plastic ones stay yellow forever.

(*She eats her cawl. BOYO watches. Then he walks over and looks in the bowl.*)

BOYO: Cawl?

MOTHER: Mmm... neck of lamb, I made a pot full of it. Are you hungry? You can have some if you want, it's still hot.

BOYO: There's nothing in the dish, Mam.

(*Pause. MOTHER looks into the bowl. Starts to laugh.*)

MOTHER: Isn't there?

(*She laughs a bit more. Suddenly she throws it to the floor.*)

MOTHER: You're right, there's nothing there.

(*Pause.*)

You know what, I've been waiting for someone to say that to me all day. Every time the nurse or the doctor comes in here for something, I've been pretending to eat my cawl, and you know what? Not one of them has told me there's nothing in it, not one of them. Do they think I don't know that, uh? What would you say, Boyo? Don't you think I know there's no cawl in there, but do they say something? No. Because they don't want to upset me because I'm mad, that's why. Tell me, Boyo, who's joking who here? And I'll tell you another thing, there's no Mr Snow either, in fact there's never been a Mr Snow. It's all a pack of lies.

(*She sits down triumphantly in the chair.*)

BOYO: How long have you been pretending then?

MOTHER: I don't know, but long enough for me to enjoy it – mad Mrs Lewis in the house of fools.

(*She laughs maniacally.*)

And some nights I howl like a sick dog, howl and bark here, and in they come with some tablets and ask me quietly to stop barking… me, a woman my age, barking? What's the world coming to? Your sister told me one day… she was scared of the dinosaurs, and then she told me not to tell you, well is that sense? It's not the dinosaurs she's afraid of, it's herself… doesn't know if she's coming or going, and you don't know either… you, Boyo, you…you told me yourself.

(*Pause.* MOTHER *has gone silent.*)

BOYO: Mam?

MOTHER: I'm still here.

BOYO: You've got to come back home.

(*Silence.*)

You hear what I'm saying?

(*Silence.*)

Say something.

(*Silence.*)

Don't stop now, Mam, please.

(*Silence.*)

MOTHER: There's a gooseberry going up and down in a lift, and a baby saying boo to a bear, and your father isn't in America.

BOYO: You've got to listen to me.

MOTHER: He's not in America I said, never went, never been, never grew a kidney bean. Now go on before I start barking, visiting's over, go back to your cell.

BOYO: You've got to tell me the truth, Mam, please.

MOTHER: The house is rocking I can tell.

BOYO: Things are changing, that's all. You were right you've got to try and get better.

MOTHER: I'll never get out of here. Where have you been living? Haven't you heard the news, everybody else has heard it?

BOYO: What news?

MOTHER: On the open cast. Some digging dinosaur has found a body up there.

BOYO: When?

MOTHER: This morning, a man's body.

BOYO: Who is it?

MOTHER: They don't know yet, but I know, and it won't be long until they find out too.

BOYO: Who is it, Mam?

(*Blackout, lights up on the open cast.* GWENNY *and* SID *approach the labourer we saw earlier.*)

SID: Oi, Clint, who is it, do you know?

LAB: Yeah, it was me who found him, I thought it was my head in the beginning.

GWENNY: But it wasn't.

LAB: No.

SID: Who is it then, local bloke?

LAB: Bloke called… Clem Lewis. Have you heard of him?

SID: What…

LAB: They reckon he's been there fifteen years.

(GWENNY *laughs hysterically.*)

SID: My old man was called Clem Lewis, must be two of them, my old man is in America.

LAB: Yeah? What's so funny then, have I said something funny?

GWENNY: You're a bad liar, that's all.

LAB: I'm not lying, they say his wife killed him.

SID: How do they know it's him?

LAB: Dental records – by his teeth. I wouldn't tell you lies. Hey, he's not your father is he?

(GWENNY *runs at him hitting out. LABOURER laughs maniacally at them.*)

(*Lights change back to the hospital.* BOYO *sits with his head in his hands.* MOTHER *takes off her hat.*)

MOTHER: Your father, I killed him, but you didn't believe

me – never went to America. True as there's no cawl in the bowl. I couldn't get the blood off the wall see, too much blue, should have been red, and if the open cast hadn't come, we'd be right. I warned you about it, I told you to be strong, to stick together, you think the house is rocking, you haven't seen nothing yet, but I tell you one thing, if you don't stand up to it, your roots are going to fly out of the ground to wherever the wind blows them.

(*Silence.* MOTHER *looks at him.*)

I don't want to see you again, Boyo.

(*Pause.*)

Kiss me goodbye, Boyo.

(*She kisses him and exits.* BOYO *looks defeated.*)

(*Lights change to the house.* SID *and* GWENNY *crawl around drunkenly to Jim Morrison's 'American Prayer'.* BOYO *enters and walks aimlessly around. Music fades.*)

SID: The police have been.

BOYO: For what?

SID: They've found his body, Boyo, on the mountain.

(*Silence.* GWENNY *is sick in the corner.*)

They think Mam killed him. But it's the wrong bloke, couldn't have been him, could it? 'Coz he's in America.

(SID *laughs, half cries in disbelief.*)

(*Lights change to a surreal court-room, where* LABOURER *plays the prosecuting council.*)

MOTHER: I killed him, is that what you want to hear?

All I know, I did it to keep us all together, under one roof, he didn't want to belong any more – if we followed him I don't know where we would have ended up, but I tell you one thing, at least my kids know who they are.

(LABOURER *enters with a torch.*)

LAB: Don't be so soft, mun. Is your name Gwen Lewis?

GWENNY: No.

LAB: Do you know who she is?

GWENNY: No.

LAB: Where were you born?

GWENNY: On the Upper West Side, New York City.

LAB: Do you know where your father is?

(*Pause.*)

GWENNY: Yes, Dodge City.

LAB: And your Mother?

GWENNY: There she is. She doesn't live with us any more.

LAB: Do you remember your father leaving?

GWENNY: No, I don't remember, I don't remember, I don't want to remember.

(*Light on* SID.)

LAB: What do you remember, mate?

SID: Are you talking to me? I can't remember, I mean it was a long time ago, but murder is murder, that's all I have to say.

(LABOURER *laughs and exits.*)

BOYO: He bought me a horse for Christmas, a toy plastic horse, I was playing with it in front of the fire, there was a lot of shouting and I was told to go upstairs. I stayed there for a long time, but then I went downstairs. The fire had gone out, and there was nobody there. I picked up my horse but my fingers went straight through him, he'd melted by the fire, and his feet were stuck to the carpet. All the way from Hong Kong to melt in a carpet in my house. Then my Mother came in and told me our father had gone to America. That's all.

MOTHER: All I know is that I've done my best, lie it might have been, but the truth hurts. If they turn out to be flotsam and I'm the Mother of flotsam, at least I know I loved them, you hear me? I loved them, that's all I've got to say.

(MOTHER *slowly walks into the darkness. Blackout.*)

(*Lights up in the house. It is a mess, strewn with cans and bottles. BOYO sits staring blankly at a TV set covered in snow. SID and GWENNY carry on oblivious, on a cocktail of drink and drugs.*)

GWENNY: They found the wrong man on the mountain, didn't they, Jack? It must have been the wrong man because he didn't have a face.

SID: And there were worms in his head.

GWENNY: And snails in his heart. Couldn't have been Dad, Jack, it couldn't have been, they made it up to make us feel bad.

SID: It was the wrong man, baby, they found the wrong man.

GWENNY: Because you knew him, didn't you?

SID: Yeah, me and him had some crazy times.

GWENNY: Clem Lewis from Dodge City.

SID: Yeah, Clem from Dodge. Stayed with him when we were 'On The Road', came looking for the dream with us, used to talk about his Joycey all the time. He said, 'I know a girl on the other side of heaven, you've got to meet her, Jack,' that's what he used to say. He said, 'You'll love her, she'll take you to dreamworld.'

(GWENNY *giggles*.)

GWENNY: Was he a good man, Jack?

SID: The best, the best.

GWENNY: Then he can't be dead, can he?

SID: Clem Lewis will never die, Joyce, never, ever.

GWENNY: So we can be happy in the house of America, Jack.

SID: Yeah… everything's fine, as we roll along this way. I am positive beyond doubt that everything will be taken care of. The thing will go along itself, and we won't go off the road, and I can sleep.

GWENNY: It's beautiful, Jack… kiss me.

(*They kiss*.)

In the heart of America with my baby Jack.

BOYO: Leave her alone, Sid.

SID: C'mon, man, I can't tell if you're dead or alive.

You've got to open your eyes, brother, you've got to let things swing. Nothing stays the same forever, get on the world's car and never get off, hitch a ride to the other side of the sun, c'mon, can't you smell the space of Iowa on the mountains, see Manhattan on TV and on our streets, play pool with a man who's seen the Chicago Bears. The world gets bigger as it gets smaller, the summer's come, brother.

GWENNY: Put this hat on.

(GWENNY *gives* BOYO *a baseball hat.*)

BOYO: Get away from me, can't you see I'm busy?

GWENNY: That's not the way it's supposed to be, you've got it on back to front.

BOYO: What is it?

GWENNY: It's a baseball hat.

BOYO: You don't play baseball, do you?

SID: You don't have to play baseball to wear the hat, man.

BOYO: Get it off, it's not my size.

GWENNY: But it suits you, it suits you.

BOYO: It's not my size, I said.

GWENNY: You can adjust it, it'll fit anybody's head, see?

BOYO: Take it back, I'm busy.

GWENNY: Don't be a spoilsport. Look there's a mirror, have a look in the mirror.

BOYO: If you don't take it, I'll throw it.

GWENNY: You could wear it anywhere.

(BOYO *scrunches it and throws it to the floor, and spits. Fade up 'Do You Know The Way To San Jose' low.* BOYO *exits.*)

GWENNY: There wasn't any need to do that. He spat on the floor too.

SID: If he doesn't want to play, we can't help him. Just think, when the sun goes down and I sit watching the long long skies over New Jersey, and sense all that raw land that rolls in one huge bulge over the West Coast.

GWENNY: And I'm sitting at the table in the exact centre of the universe, with some bourbon and my Jack talking about living and dying and freedom. Make me happy, Jack.

(*Laughter.*)

SID: Are you wearing black stockings, Joyce?

(*She nods.*)

I like black stockings on virgins, Joyce.

GWENNY: Make me happy, Jack.

SID: When will I get to feel them, baby?

GWENNY: When you tell me 'I love you'.

SID: I love you, I want to feel your skin like ripe earth.

GWENNY: Will you marry me, Jack?

SID: Yeah, when will it be?

GWENNY: Now, now, there's no time like now.

SID: I could eat you, Joycey.

GWENNY: Then eat me, lover.

SID: All good things take time.

GWENNY: Are you really Jack Kerouac?

SID: Look in my face, can you see the truth in my face?

(GWENNY *looks and nods.*)

Feel.

GWENNY: I love you, Jack.

(*They kiss.* BOYO *enters and watches.*)

BOYO: Leave her alone, Sid.

GWENNY: Who's that?

SID: Nothing, nobody.

GWENNY: Come and make us a baby, Jack, a sweet pea dream baby that runs in the Florida sun in winter, sleeps all night and smiles all day: a baby to be proud of, a baby to sing and dance and fly in the air. Come and roll over me and write poems on my belly. How many b's in baby? I love you, I love you.

(SID *and* GWENNY *undress and make love in front of a red fire as music plays.* BOYO *watches for a while then exits. He returns with a club. Suddenly he attacks.*)

BOYO: Leave her alone, you bastard.

(*A violent fight ensues, ending with all the furniture and props rearranged. It ends with* GWENNY *smashing a bottle over* BOYO's *head.* SID *and* GWENNY *exit. Blackout. Silence. Lights up slowly on* BOYO, *sitting in a pool of light, smoking.*)

BOYO: There is... a house... in New Orleans... they call... the rising sun... Jack Kerouac... Joyce Johnson, Allen Ginsberg... No Allen.

(*Lights up in house.* GWENNY *sits alone.*)

BOYO: Gwenny?

GWENNY: You talking to me?

BOYO: It's me, Gwenny, Boyo.

GWENNY: I don't know you.

BOYO: You all right?

GWENNY: I've got morning sickness.

BOYO: We've got to get out of the house, Gwenny.

GWENNY: Stop calling me that.

BOYO: Come with me, we've got to get out, come on.

GWENNY: I know you, you're the spoilsport.

BOYO: Come on you need some air, come for a walk with me.

GWENNY: I don't walk with strangers.

BOYO: Give me your hand.

GWENNY: Don't touch me.

(*Pause.*)

You want to take my baby from me, don't you?

BOYO: Baby?

GWENNY: We're going to have a baby, me and Jack.

BOYO: He's your brother.

GWENNY: Don't try and fool me whoever you are. If you want to leave the house, you go, but we're staying here.

BOYO: I don't believe you.

GWENNY: We're thinking of calling the baby Dodge, what do you think?

BOYO: I don't, Gwenny.

(BOYO *exits. Fade up Patti Smith's 'Because The Night' as* SID *enters the house. He looks at* GWENNY. *There is a long silence.*)

GWENNY: I'm going to have a baby, Jack.

SID: Oh yeah? Big or small, or medium, how would you like it done, madam?

GWENNY: It's true, Jack, a love baby... I can feel it... a love baby.

SID: Any chance of coffee?

GWENNY: I'm not lying, you know I've been sick, it's morning sickness, happens when you're pregnant.

(SID *laughs.*)

What are you laughing at?

SID: You, huh, it's a joke, innit?

GWENNY: I'm not, Jack, it's true.

SID: You're drunk, you need a bath.

GWENNY: No, I want to talk to you, about the baby.

SID: You're not having one.

GWENNY: I am, I am, why don't you believe me, I love you, Jack, I wouldn't lie to you.

(SID *looks at her, slowly realising what she's saying.*)

SID: Hey come on, don't play games.

GWENNY: Give me a hug, Jack, you're supposed to kiss me and tell me I'm the best woman in the world. Tell me you're happy, please tell me you're happy.

SID: Oh, fucking hell… get away from me…

(GWENNY *tries to hug him but he pushes her away.*)

GWENNY: Jack, I love you, we've made a baby, say you're happy.

SID: You're not having one.

(*Silence.*)

GWENNY: Do you want a drink?

(*Passes him a bottle, but he throws it away.*)

Do you want to go to bed and play then? Why don't you smile?

SID: Because you're my sister, you understand me?

GWENNY: No, you're not.

SID: I am, I am, game's over, Gwenny.

GWENNY: Gwenny? Who's Gwenny?

SID: Listen to me.

(*Pause.*)

Remember the books, I read and you read, about Jack

Kerouac and Joyce Johnson.

GWENNY: A love story.

SID: Yeah, a love story. We liked it, remember, and remember things were going wrong, like when I didn't get the job on the open cast, and Mam was ill?

GWENNY: The dinosaurs, we ran away from them.

SID: Yeah, and even since we were small, Mam told us that Dad was in America, and you were writing letters to him, and we thought he'd ask us to go out and see him?

GWENNY: No.

SID: Say you do, you do. I said I was Jack, and you were Joyce.

GWENNY: No, but I know you're Jack and I'm Joyce.

SID: No, it was a game, a game you hear me? It was a game, we were upset, we believed it for a bit, but in the back of our minds we knew we were only playing, didn't we?

GWENNY: No Jack, I'm not playing – game, what game?

(SID *is exasperated.*)

SID: Your name is Gwen, Gwenny Lewis.

(*Silence.*)

And I'm your brother, Sid Lewis, and your other brother isn't here, but we call him Boyo, don't we?

(GWENNY *shakes her head and stares at him.*)

GWENNY: Your name is Jack Kerouac, and you'll be with me forever. Why are you trying to confuse me?

SID: Let's talk about the baby, is it true you're going to have a baby?

GWENNY: Of course it's true, I wouldn't lie, I love you.

SID: Oh Jesus.

GWENNY: You don't love me, do you?

SID: I love you, Gwenny, but you're my sister, can't you see that?

GWENNY: Stop playing this game with me, I don't like it, you're being odd, I don't like it.

(SID *puts his arm around her.*)

SID: It's all lies, Gwenny, it's dreamland.

GWENNY: There's nothing wrong with that, I knew you'd take me there.

SID: What can I do, what can I do?

GWENNY: Just say you love me, Jack.

SID: Don't call me Jack, I'm not Jack, I never was Jack, and I'm not Jack now.

GWENNY: But I'm going to have your baby.

SID: It's fucking dream city, can't you see that?

GWENNY: Don't be ugly.

SID: I'm being ugly, because it is fucking ugly.

GWENNY: Don't swear.

SID: We've got to get rid of it, you've got to see a doctor.

GWENNY: No, no doctors.

SID: He can help us.

GWENNY: No doctors, they'll kill my baby.

SID: It's the only way.

GWENNY: No, get away from me, what's happened to you, Jack?

SID: It's wrong, Gwenny, I…

(*Grabbing her.*)

GWENNY: Get off me you're hurting the baby.

SID: We've got to get rid of it, Gwenny.

(GWENNY *hits him hard across the face.* SID *pushes her away.*)

It's not all my fault, it's your fault too, but we've had it now, you hear me, we've had it.

GWENNY: You're a fraud.

SID: Boyo. Don't go out of the house you hear me, till I come back. He'll get a doctor, he'll help me, he's my brother, no babies, no way.

(GWENNY *scorns him as drums and crashing cymbals play.*)

GWENNY: You're a fucking fraud.

(*Lights change. BOYO stands alone among some ruins. SID approaches behind him. During the scene, BOYO can hardly look at his brother.*)

SID: Boyo.

(*BOYO turns round, looks at him.*)

BOYO: Sid. (*Flatly.*)

SID: Yeah, it's me.

(*Pause.*)

BOYO: How's Gwenny?

SID: She's still in the house.

(*Pause.*)

BOYO: She told me she was pregnant, Sid.

SID: She's lying.

BOYO: She said it was yours.

SID: I told you it's lies.

BOYO: You haven't touched her, have you?

SID: No, she's in the house.

BOYO: Look at me, you bastard.

(BOYO *grabs him.*)

SID: It's all finished.

(*Pause.* BOYO *releases him.*)

You've got to help me, Boyo. Gwenny says she's pregnant, she says it's me. What the fuck can I do, you've got to help me, Boyo?

BOYO: Get off me, get off, it's all fucked, all of it.

SID: You're not listening to me. I thought it was a game, Boyo, a game, but I didn't know. Gwenny, she can't see it, she thinks she's Joyce.

BOYO: Are you trying to tell me you were playing, that all the mad things that have been going on for the last few months was playing, what the fuck you take me for, uh?

SID: It's the truth, it was the shock, the old man, and then Mam. And I was pissed all the time, I didn't know what I was doing.

(BOYO *grabs him*.)

BOYO: I'll tell you what you did, you slept with your own sister, you got me? You told me lie after lie, you bastard, and now you turn round to me and say, you didn't know what was going on? All the fucking dreaming, and the yankage, and you say you were playing? Get off me.

SID: It's the truth, I didn't know who I was. I did think I was Jack for a bit, felt good. I'm fucking finished, that's why. I'm on the scrap heap, I'm nearly thirty, Boyo, and the only job I've ever had is fucking gravedigging.

(*Pause*.)

Jack had all the answers, we were on the same wavelength, but I didn't think it would turn out like this, and I don't know if she is pregnant, she won't see a doctor, Boyo. You've got to help me, she doesn't know it was a game.

BOYO: Can't you see what you've done to us you sick bastard?

(*Pushes him away*.)

SID: We messed about a bit, Boyo, that's all, I don't…

BOYO: That's all? She doesn't know who she is.

SID: It was the way she was dressing, she was driving me

mad, she was Joyce, but I didn't Boyo, we never made it, we were always drinking. I've tried to tell her I'm Sid but she won't believe me… she still thinks she's in America or somewhere, she's not joking, Boyo. Why doesn't she stop and say she's Gwenny, why Boyo, why? Help me, Boyo, I'm your brother.

BOYO: Not any more you're not.

(BOYO *kicks* SID *in the groin, punches him.* SID *hardly puts a hand out to stop him. To the music of Lou Reed's 'Perfect Day',* BOYO *strangles his brother.* SID *dies.* BOYO *drags him off, weeping.*)

(*Lights up on* GWENNY, *walking round the room unsteadily with a bottle of tablets still in her hands.*)

GWENNY: And he said in Iowa I know by now the children must be crying in the land where they let the children cry, and tonight the stars will be out… and God is Pooh Bear.

(*She laughts then stops suddenly.*)

Why did he say the children cry?

(*Pause.*)

Jack was a fraud, but I'll have the baby that will laugh and laugh forever.

(*Pause.*)

No I wont, he's gone to get a doctor, he wants to kill the baby, I won't let him come too far now, oops.

(*Pause.*)

He's left me on my own.

(*Silence.*)

I used to cry when I was younger.

(GWENNY *pops a load of pills.*)

The truth of it is he said he was a poet.

(*Silence.*)

I was born in a crowd now I'll die on my own.

(*She falls over.*)

Take the chains off your feet, brother… kiss me… kiss me. Got to get our of here fast, baby, I've got the Benzedrine, nice sweets. Too many sweets, I'm sick.

(*She vomits.*)

Where's my Dad and Mam, make me better… gone, all without me, always run away… no home, no… I'm all right, Jack.

(*She drinks again and take more pills, and vomits.*)

We can go out in the moonlight when the dinosaurs are sleeping. They've eaten the dragon, and found my father… tin men… clankety clank… boom buddy boom… budddy hiccup clanks… the wind will make them feel better.

(*Silence.*)

(*She tries to get up.*)

Oh… my feet are like lead, look… all pins and needles… won't be long now… I can't get up… and now's my chance when the world's asleep, but my legs won't walk, won't run, look at them, all those thousands of miles down my leg… the plains of Iowa, the girls from the prairie got a ladder in her stocking, stairway to Heaven, my belly will grow like a new mountain, it will have climbers on it, I'm conquered forever... all creepy with hard hands and fingers... get off me... get him off me... GET HIM OFF ME...

(*Silence.*)

All quiet in a forgotten town... music I need... I'll have to lie on the bed... but Jack will be there and he'll want to breed with me...

(BOYO *enters in darkness.*)

BOYO: Gwenny?

GWENNY: Here he comes, the breeder, who doesn't want to know. I'm keeping my baby, go away, if you've come to kill it.

BOYO: Gwenny?

GWENNY: I can't feel my arms. Please mister, can you tell me... why I can't... move? You want my breast, Jack, suck if you like but save some for the baby...

BOYO: Help me, Gwenny.

GWENNY: Is it... raining?

(*Pause.*)

I think I'm going to... all lost... my way... you know... Sssleep...

BOYO: Gwenny!

(BOYO *holds her tightly. Lights fade slowly to blackout.*)

THE END

'Coal the dole and heaps of Soul. *House of America* is an honest triumph.'

NME

'Terrific...achingly well acted for those who like their meat raw.'

Daily Telegraph

'This is a universal soul-mate for anyone who has experienced the angst of an untrendy upbringing in a drab place. Mesmerising.'

Buzz

'Nothing prepared us for the explosion of angst, guilt and cultural concern of *House of America*...

The Guardian

1989

Cath Tregenna, Russ Gomer and Sharon Morgan. Photoshoot Cardiff Bay 1988

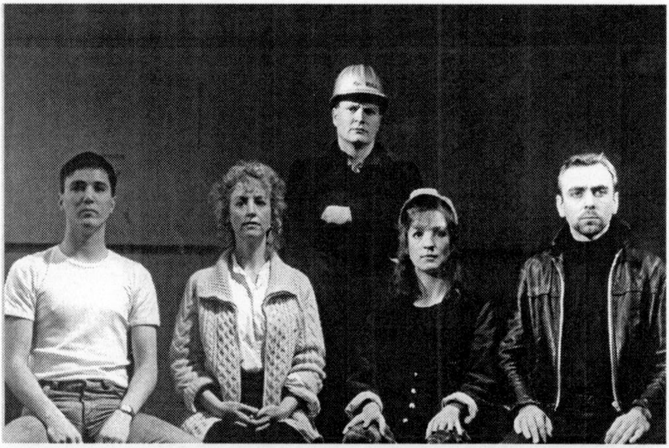

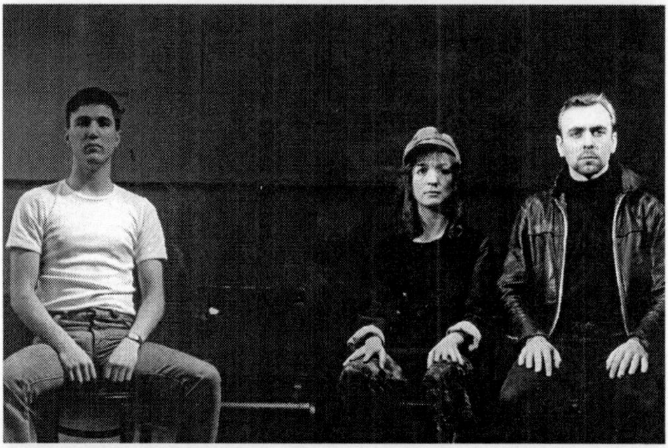

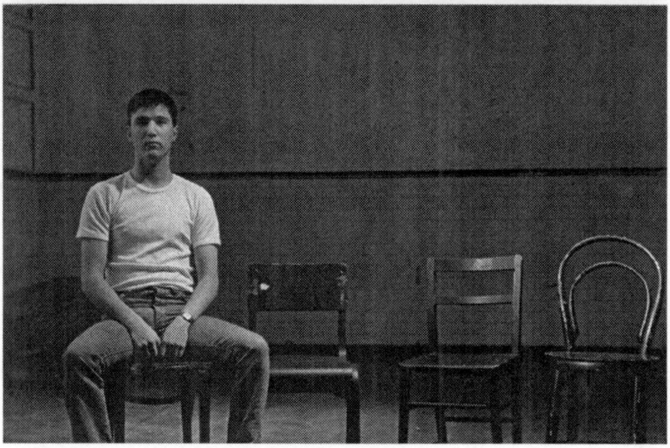

1989

The family and other chairs 1989, Boyo (Richard Lynch) Mam (Sharon Morgan) Labourer (Wyndham Price) Gwenny (Kath Treganna) Sid (Russ Gomer)

1989

"Your father's not in America. Never went, never been, never grew a kidney bean"

1989

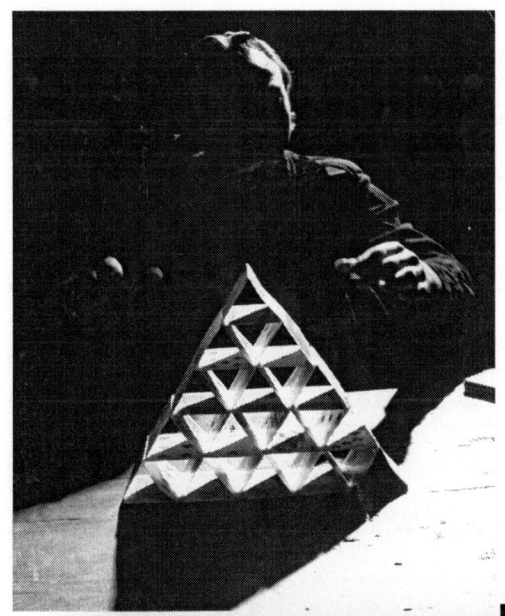

"Don't believe everything you see"

1989

Rehearsal rooms Chapter October 1989

1992

"We can go out in the moonlight when the dinosaurs are sleeping"

1992

1992

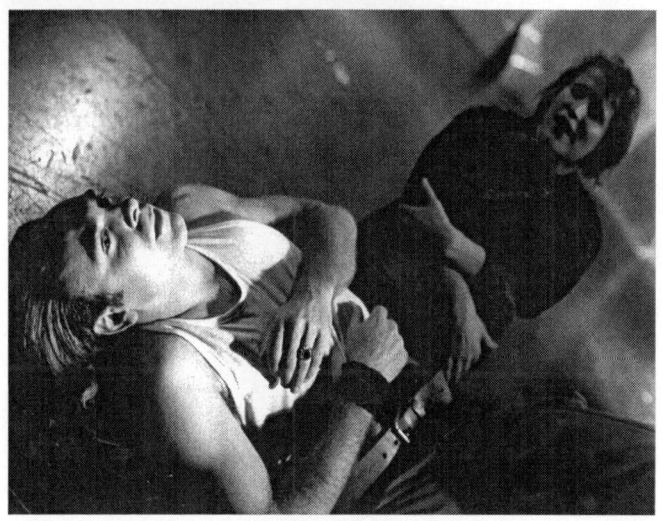

Lisa Palfrey (Gwenny) Russ Gomer (Sid) Rhodri Hugh (Boyo) UK tour 1992.

1997

The family on the road 1997. (Boyo) Richard Harrington (Sid) Jâms Thomas (Gwenny) Shelley Rees (Mam) Helen Griffin. UK and Australia tour.

1997

1997

"Fancy going on the road in Boyo's car? Wouldn't get you as far as Pembroke!"

1997

"He was a dreamer and he fell for the glitter."

1997

Original flyer and poster printed with Johnny Greco's help in a basement on New Cavendish St London 1988.

Photoshoot Abercrave 1992 with Russ Gomer.

LOOKING BACK

Sharon Morgan.............Mam
Russel Gomer................Sid
Richard Lynch...............Boyo

SHARON MORGAN – MAM, 1988

Recently I have been asked to remember seminal moments in my career with ever increasing frequency. Maybe distance lends enchantment or I persuade myself that it endows the brain with a certain objectivity, but I certainly find the process useful and indeed quite entertaining.

Ed and I were playing brother and sister in *Pobl Y Cwm* twenty years ago when he asked me if I would like to play the part of Mam in *House of America*. There would be no money and it was to be a part of Moving Being's Spring season at St Stephen's, now The Point, run by the visionary Geoff Moore. I had seen and indeed read *When the river runs dry*, Ed's previous play, which was performed at the Made in Wales new writing festival Write on. I had been involved with new writing through this company and many others for many years. I also loved a challenge and believed strongly (and still do!) that lucrative and mostly tedious television work should subsidise stuff that was worth doing, that said something important and exciting about life and people in Wales, which in 1988 was a country struggling implausibly, and some might say hopelessly, to recreate itself in a way suitable for the late 20th century. *House of America*, it seemed to me, encapsulated the tragic desperation of unfulfilled potential and did so poetically and with humour. I wasn't so sure however that the play would work, I thought maybe it needed cutting or clarification here and there, that maybe it rambled too much at times.

Indeed, it was by no means clear when we turned up, Cath Tregenna, Tim Lyn, Russ Gomer, Wyndham Price, Ed and myself for that first read through that this was going to be maybe the most successful theatre production that I had been part of, that it would capture the imagination of the Welsh artistic community and beyond, win many prizes for Ed, and that it would be reprised in several more incarnations.

We were fairly mad in 1988. We drank and smoked a lot, there were always five packets of Silk Cut on the small black table centre stage, that with the two chairs and one flat comprised the set. The budget was fifty pounds a production, for this was part of a season of plays, and we were all to appear in Howard Barker's *No End of Blame* after this. So no money, at all! Done for the love of it, for the fun of it. We sourced our own costumes based on our reading of our characters, subject to Ed's approval, which he gave us. I chose an old black skirt of my mother's from the 30s, a big Arran-knit cardigan bought in Ireland a decade old, and a pair of black slip-on shoes about half a size too big.

It proved to be an artistic leap for me. Ed wanted to break the walls down, he didn't want us to approach the creation of these characters in a conventional way. It was very important to him that there was nothing stifled or held back about the style of the playing. I needed to rethink my careful detailed cautious technique and replace it with something more instinctive. Although I recognised that all the work of the previous twenty years was still there under the surface, it was a process of freeing the subconscious more consciously if you like, of trusting my instinct more, of not letting anything hold me back, of experimenting and thinking afresh, of taking risks. We could do it, we were working for nothing in an old church down the docks, we could do what we liked, we could do something daring that was going to change the world, which is of course the point.

It was extremely frightening, terrifying in fact. Every night was different, the blocking was more or less the same, the dialogue was the same but the character's inner life was truly recreated during every performance which is exhausting. Of course Mam is mad, she doesn't think so but every one else does. It is a case of the mad being sane. Mam sees clearly and sanely, and this in itself made this approach even trickier, creating her reality, maintaining a clear through line required tremendous discipline within the freedom, so that there was no danger of it becoming 'mad acting', or self indulgent in any way. What of course was wonderful for a middle - aged actress, (well 38, but really an actress of any age then and now) was that Mam had beliefs and convictions and she ACTED on them! This was a good part, an important character with good lines, with heart and soul, who actually affects the action of the play. Parts of violent women who act on their convictions are pretty hard to come by.

Ed was an inspiration, he believed totally in what he was trying to create, and took us along with him, he knew exactly what he was trying to do, or at least gave a very good impression of it! On the first night twelve people came, including the playwright Sion Eirian, who was quoted as saying Ed might as well throw away his pencil (Well it was a long time ago!), meaning, of course that Ed would never write anything half as good again (Discuss!) and that amazingly talented actor who was to play the lead in *No End of Blame* Dorien Thomas, who was completely blown over. The audiences built and built over the next week and the reaction was uniformly effusive. Ed rewrote a little, adding that wonderfully funny speech for Mam at the beginning, and we toured (with Richard Lynch playing Boyo this time) in the Autumn in Wales and the Battersea arts centre, and in 1989 we went to the Edinburgh Festival.

At Edinburgh we also performed Ed's first Welsh language play *Adar Heb Adenydd*. This was a play which lent itself to far more creative improvisational techniques than *House Of America*. Indeed I would make up a different, and I mean a different character every night, without changing the dialogue! And who she was depended on who I was that day, that night. It was a lot of fun. With *Adar Heb Adenydd* the performing of it seemed crucial, and I think that explains the fact that sometimes it worked and sometimes it didn't. I remember sitting in a taxi on the way to perform it at the Edinburgh Festival and discussing how to make it foolproof, not that any play is of course, but we thought that if we could only find that key, turn that switch. I also remember one night on tour in Carmarthen when Ed berated the men during the interval, saying, like some sort of crazed rugby coach 'Come on boys, even the girls are getting more laughs than you tonight' which left Cath Tregenna and myself both bemused and rather pleased.

The gender issue raised its head for me again during rehearsals for *The Myth Of Michael Roderick*. This we performed as part of another season at St Stephen's, together with *Largo Desolato* by Vaclav Havel. *Myth of Michael Roderick* was an English language version of *Adar Heb Adenydd*. It was very loosely based, and felt much wilder and more aggressive, and my character, Betty, had changed considerably. When I argued that 'A woman wouldn't do this' Ed replied in true Marks and Spencer form 'This is not just any woman but a woman I have created'. It proved to be a turning point in my career as I realised that I would have to start writing my own plays.

RUSSEL GOMER – SID LEWIS

Playing Sid Lewis in the very first production of *House of America* was not only a great honour and a tremendous experience, it was also a sort of actor's epiphany for me.

When the project began I'd been 'out and about' in the profession for several years. I'd learnt a few tricks of the trade and honed, a little, some of the technical skills I'd first practised at drama college. I was physically able and had what I considered to be a decent sense of timing. I was champing at the bit for new roles. Yeah. Bring it on!

After the first week of rehearsals however, I realised, much to my chagrin, that if I was to do Sid Lewis any justice, it would require a great deal more than just the suite of performance skills that I had brought along to the 'House'. It was the sheer power of the play that hit me. The depths of tragedy, straight out of ancient Greece but in the here and now! It was the intense ache, both sweet and sad, one feels for the family, their banter, their love and insanity. It was the humour and the darkness and that sense of impending doom. Amongst all this, the characters needed to be played with a great vitality. Immense commitment and a huge passion were essential, I realised!

With Ed Thomas' brilliant and dynamic direction and inspired by those wonderful actors who stepped into that world with me and under the spell of the play itself, I found that commitment and that passion.

It was at that moment that I consider myself to have become an actor.

For that rite and for the bonds of friendship I made then, I am truly grateful.

RICHARD LYNCH – BOYO

Simon McBurney asserts in Theatre Complicite's *Mnemonic* that 're-membering is essentially not only an act of retrieval but a creative thing, it happens in the moment, it's an act, an act... of the imagination'. If this is true then perhaps what I remember from our production of *House of America* never happened at all. Maybe I'm just making it up. Recollections chiselled and shaped by time into something other. And that would be about right because that in it's essence is what Y Cwmni was about... a wilful act of the imagination.

A black table and chair... Wyndham losing a drumstick and muttering such a savage expletive it made us laugh for years... tiger balm for my elbow... breaking Gomers' nose in Carmarthen... using the vicars' cut-glass fruit bowl as an ashtray in one of the post show soirées... Mars then us in the Butcher's Arms... all the way to Spain to pick a team like that... sleeping anywhere and everywhere... Sharon uncontrollable after the theft of her costume from Ed's car in Brixton... laughing like drains...

That's how it was. *House* was the beginning of a creative journey that would last a decade and forge some of the finest work I've ever done. Where rhythm and word were so in tune they created a muscular theatre that inspired and challenged wherever we played. I am immensely proud to have been a part of it.

Carlyle from *Song from a Forgotten City* hits the nail on the head... 'wouldn't it be good to have a pure memory... a pure recollection of good things that have happened man, that are like sweet. Like friends.'

And it was sweet. It really was.

PARTHIAN

Drama Titles

ISBN	Price	Title	Author
9781905762811	9.99	*Black Beach*	Coca, Jordi; Casas, Joan; Cunillé, Lluïsa, Teare, Jeff (ed.)
9781905762859	7.99	*Blink*	Rowlands, Ian
9781902638966	7.99	*Butterfly*	Rowlands, Ian
9781902638539	6.99	*Football*	Davies, Lewis
9781905762590	9.99	*Fuse*	Jones, Patrick
9781902638775	7.99	*Hijinx Theatre*	Cullen, Greg; Morgan, Sharon; Davies, Lewis; Hill, Val (ed.)
9781906998547	8.99	*House of America*	Thomas, Ed
9780952155867	6.99	*Merthyr Trilogy, The*	Osborne, Alan
9781902638416	7.99	*More Lives than One*	Jenkins, Mark
9781902638799	7.99	*Mother Tongue*	Williams, Roger
9780952155874	6.99	*New Welsh Drama 1*	Malik, Afshan; Williams, Roger; Davies, Lewis, Teare, Jeff (ed.)
9781902638133	5.99	*New Welsh Drama 2*	Evans, Siân; Smith, Othniel; Williams, Roger; Teare, Jeff (ed.)
9781902638355	7.99	*New Welsh Drama 3*	Ross, Lesley; Davies, Lewis; Morgan, Chris (ed.)
9781902638485	9.99	*Now You're Talking*	Davies, Hazel Walford (ed.)
9781908069962	8.99	*Protagonists, The*	Chamberlain, Brenda; Davies, Damian Walford (ed.)
9781902638638	7.99	*Seeing Without Light*	Turley, Simon
9781902638249	9.99	*Selected Work '95-'98*	Thomas, Ed
9781906998363	7.99	*State of Nature*	Turley, Simon
9781902638669	7.99	*Still Life*	Way, Charles
9781906998585	9.99	*Strange Case of Dr Jekyll and Mr Hyde as Told to Carl Jung by an Inmate of Broadmoor Asylum, The*	Mark, Ryan
9781909844681	8.99	*Tonypandemonium*	Trezise, Rachel
9781902638478	7.99	*Transitions: New Welsh Drama IV*	Morgan, Chris (ed.)
9781902638010	6.99	*Trilogy of Appropriation, A*	Rowlands, Ian

PARTHIAN

Story
The Library of Wales short story anthology
VOLUME 2 EDITED BY DAI SMITH

Story
The Library of Wales short story anthology
VOLUME 1 EDITED BY DAI SMITH

The Autobiography of a Super-tramp
W.H. DAVIES

A Kingdom
JAMES HANLEY

LIBRARY OF WALES

www.thelibraryofwales.com
www.parthianbooks.com

PARTHIAN

BRENDA CHAMBERLAIN
The Protagonists
Edited by Damian Walford Davies

DRAMA

THE VISITOR
KATHERINE STANSFIELD

FICTION

CRAIG HAWES
The WITCH DOCTOR *of* UMM SUQEIM

POETRY

You, Me and the Birds
Alan Kellermann

www.parthianbooks.com